A … backs.
NIG… els for
women – a new kind of love story.

NIGHTSHADES

SHOCKWAVES *by Thomas Tessier*
TAKEOVER *by Rosalind Ashe*
FLASHBACK *by Julia Greene*
AFTER LOUISE *by Teresa Crane*
BELLA DONNA *by Eden Carroll*
FORGET-ME-NOT *by Emily Mapleston*
FOREVER *by Margaret Pemberton*
FIRE DANCE *by Caroline Graham*
FAIR DEAL *by Eden Carroll*
DOUBLE PORTRAIT *by Flora Fraser*
PRETTY WOMAN *by Julia Swift*
TIME AGAIN *by Carol Trent*
DARLING KATE *by Teresa Crane*
DISTANT LOVE *by Mary Cartwright*
DARK GEMINI *by Judith Rothman*
JACK-IN-THE-GREEN *by Clo Chapman*

NIGHTSHADES

Teresa Crane

DARLING KATE

FONTANA PAPERBACKS

First published by Fontana Paperbacks 1983

Made and printed in Great Britain by
William Collins Sons & Co. Ltd., Glasgow

PROLOGUE

She stood quite still at the top of the dark sweep of the staircase, her child's figure dwarfed by mahogany bannisters of massive proportions, sinisterly shadowed. Around her the house, empty, decaying, dim-lit from shuttered windows, awaited with her the moment of discovery. Her heart pounded, the faint nausea of delightedly fearful excitement stirred her stomach.

Beneath her, in the hall, there was a glimmering scuffle of movement, then stillness.

'Kate?' The voice was a boy's, imperious, light, unbroken. Only she could detect the faint note of uncertainty, of half-angry unease. 'Kate . . . where are you? Come on, now. Don't be stupid . . .' the boy stepped into the barred pattern of light which trellised the bare, dirty floorboards as the sun shone through a boarded window. He glanced up, brilliant eyes in a narrow, clever face catching the light and gleaming like dark diamonds. 'Kate!'

Caught in the compulsion of the moment she stood like a statue, her small face screwed up in excited, silent laughter.

The boy wandered uncertainly back the way he had come. 'Kate, for goodness' sake . . . what are you playing at? We're wasting time . . .' he paused, waiting. 'Stupid thing. I'm leaving.' All sound and movement stopped. Kate strained her ears as around her golden dust motes swirled and settled in the bright blades of light that knifed the lofty spaces of the derelict house.

Surely . . . he hadn't really gone?

Very, very quietly she tiptoed to the great double doors of the ballroom. A floorboard creaked beneath her foot. She froze. The silence deepened. She shivered a little; the shadowed space was cold after the summer warmth outside. Like a small, brown mouse she scuttled to the tall window, peered through a crack in the shutters. The two horses that she and Stephen had been riding still cropped contentedly on what had once been the sweeping lawns of the great house. Stephen was still here then. Her heart beat a little slower. She hadn't really wanted to make him angry. It was only a game. She would have hated it if he had left her . . .

She stood on tiptoe, pressing her face to the crack, trying to widen her field of vision. Where was he? What was he doing? One of the horses, the big bay called Rainstorm, who was her favourite, lifted his head for a moment, as if sensing her eyes upon him. He was a magnificent animal, the personal mount of Mrs Erskine who ran the riding school that was housed in the old stable block, and Kate was the only one apart from Mrs Erskine herself who was allowed to ride him – a privilege of which she was justly proud. He ran like the wind, jumped like a cat. She could still feel the wild lift of excitement when she had set him, a few minutes ago, at the 'Devil's Leap', still hear Stephen's shout as he had seen what she was about to do.

She grinned a quick, happy grin. Stephen – clever, imaginative, resourceful Stephen – was the unchallenged ringleader of almost all that the two of them did. Whenever they met, beneath the great old tree at the back of the house – the house that was their playground and their own personal world – it was always Stephen who would have ready the idea for a new and wonderful game, or the beginning of a glorious story upon which they would act and elaborate through the long summer evenings. Kate did not mind his dominance, was in fact more than ready freely to grant his superiority in most things. But it gave her, always, a small, sweet satisfaction to know that on the back of a horse she was more than his equal, that she could indeed frighten him with her skill and her apparently reckless exploits; could, in this one activity, actually outdo him. It was because he had not dared the difficult jump across the lane and had had to go the long way round that she had reached the house first today and had, on impulse, hidden from him. But . . . where was he now . . . ?

'Got you!'

She went rigid with shock, leapt, shrieking, back from the window. 'Stephen! You beast! You . . . you . . .' she stammered to a halt, trying to calm the awful racing of her heart. Cold sweat prickled her skin uncomfortably. 'You frightened me!'

'Serves you right for playing stupid games.' Dismissively, he turned from her, towards the tall, half-open doors. 'Silly baby, playing baby games . . .'

'I'm not! I'm not a baby!'

He stopped at the tremor in her voice, turned back,

narrowing his eyes against the slatted light. He was a tall boy, lightly built and graceful. She loved him more than anything in the world; knew with clear, childish certainty that she would love him until the day that she died.

'I'm not a baby,' she repeated, more calmly.

His bad temper evaporated. With a smile like sunshine he reached a hand to her. 'Of course you aren't. You're my little Kate. My darling Kate. I was just mad because you hid from me, and I couldn't find you . . .'

'You did, though. I was afraid you'd gone, and left me. But you didn't. You found me . . .'

He reached a thin hand to tug gently the long, untidy plait of dark, shining hair which hung across her shoulder. His eyes were deadly serious, his boy's voice light. 'Silly Kate. As if I'd have left you here, alone. As if I'd leave you anywhere alone. Ever.'

CHAPTER ONE

It sounded as if vandals were loose in the flat upstairs.

Kate Richards, curled comfortably in an enormous armchair before the fire, swore under her breath in an extremely unladylike way and stuck her fingers in her ears, trying to return with grim concentration to her book, reading the same paragraph unsuccessfully for at least the third time.

There came from above her head another crash, followed by a series of thumps, a shriek, and a sudden shout of laughter.

Kate snapped the book shut with an aggressively sharp movement and exasperatedly tossed it onto the floor beside the chair. This, heaven help her, was supposed to be a quiet holiday at home. A week's peace after hectic months of work that had barely given her time to notice that Christmas had come and gone. When she had planned it, however, deciding against the more populous attractions of the West Indies or North Africa she had not, understandably, taken into account the arrival of new – and from the sound of it devastatingly noisy – neighbours.

A child's voice called and a woman's, more quietly,

answered. Kate got up and, in an attempt to smooth her ruffled nerves, wandered to the tall window. She never tired of this view of the park, winter or summer. When the trees were in leaf the distant lake glinted tantalisingly through a thick curtain of verdant colour; at this time of the year, on a clear, chill day such as today it lay like a sheet of silver beyond the dark lace of the bare trees, its surface reflecting the wide, cold, pastel sky, the green of the parkland brilliant around it. By a trick of the rolling countryside Cravensford, five miles or so distant, looked still a market town set in a fold of the Hertfordshire countryside, and the church spire and old roofs of what little could be seen of Sheldon, the once-village from which this lovely old house took its name, gave the impression of the hamlet set in woodland that it had once been, as if the house itself had preserved this ancient view for its own. In fact, as Kate knew, nothing could be farther from the truth. The 'twenties and 'thirties had seen, here as elsewhere, the march of rank upon rank of identical, undistinguished houses across the countryside from the little town to the surrounding villages, enveloping them in an urban, featurelessly ugly sea of bricks, mortar, granite paving stones and clipped privet hedges. The 'sixties building boom, with its updated windows and cedar cladding had finished the job, bringing more new estates, acres of them, to mantle and smother the few green fields and hillsides that had been left, to impose its maze of streets and closes with improbable names upon copses, meadows and streams. Cravensford now was simply a town like any other town; busy, bustling, soulless, jammed with traffic, with a surfeit of supermarkets and shoe shops, and possessing a lack of atmosphere that could be attributed as much to the so-called town planners as to the petrol fumes and sodium lights of a modern, over-populated area. Only distant views now, such as this from Sheldon Hall, could dress it deceptively in peace and charm. As for the village of Sheldon – it had long ago been absorbed into this urban sprawl, and a motorist driving from Cravensford to the motorway might pass through the High Street and never realise that here, once, had stood a pretty village, a community in its own right since Saxon times. He might notice the sixteenth century merchant's house that still stood on the corner of Church Street, or glimpse through the trees the church itself, with its square Norman tower crowned by the graceful spire of another century. He might glance at the littered patch of grass that once had been that centre of village life, the green, and upon which still stood a massive, rusted iron pump, suitably fenced in and labelled, or at the lopsided row of little cottages that supported each other, as they had for upwards of four centuries, at the bend of the High Street. But these things were commonplace this close to London, where greed and the internal combustion engine had taken over all but the most fortunate small corners, and merited not much more than that single, fleeting glance. What the traveller would not see was the old house, Sheldon Hall, which nestled still, incredibly, in its parkland just beyond the village, a monument to times gone by adapted with grace to the needs of today. From the windows of the old mansion, where Kate now stood, the contours of the land and the remnants of what had once been a royal hunting forest disguised and softened the changes wrought by years of swift development and it took only a little imagination to see the past almost as clearly as the present. She and Stephen had stood a thousand times at this window – never dreaming then that it could ever become their own – peopling the overgrown park and its all but derelict outbuildings with the shadows of history, graphically described and enthusiastically romanticised. As she stood now, almost she could see the two children they had been, refugees from the uninspiring semi-detached houses and the straight, tarmacked streets, racing across the grassland towards the tangled jungle of woodland that then had ringed the stagnant, scummed waters of the lake . . .

She turned abruptly away, the familiar pain moving in her; no longer, perhaps, that agonising, knife-like pain that once she had thought she might die of, but a dull ache, a bruise bruised again, an old companion and one she knew now would never leave her. Almost without volition she walked to the marble mantlepiece where his picture stood: a child no longer, but a tall, dark young man, slim, straight, thin-faced, with dark, untidy hair and compelling eyes. From the silver frame he watched her, as he always did, with that secret, changing, intimate look that brought him, whole, into the room beside her. Dead these three years, in this photograph he lived again. Stephen, she asked, as she had asked so often before, Stephen, where are you? Why don't you come, as we both always said we would? Why don't you? Is it that you are here, and I can't see you, hear you? Or is it, truly that there is nothing beyond this . . . ?

She nearly jumped out of her skin as above her head someone dragged a heavy piece of furniture across the floor and the glass chandelier swung dangerously. When the great old house had been converted into flats, an extra floor had been built into the height of the enormous ballroom. Kate's flat – that had been hers and Stephen's for the last two years of their married life – incorporated the ballroom itself, where they had played so often as youngsters. When Stephen had heard of the project nothing would suit him but that they should live here, where so much of their young lives had been spent, where they had been friends and childish comrades, hesitant, adolescent sweethearts and, finally, lovers in every sense of the word. And the only apartment that he would consider, though at the time it had meant stretching their financial resources almost to breaking point, had been the most splendid, with its original fireplaces and its views across the magnificent parkland, now restored and carefully husbanded. The ballroom had been cleverly partitioned into sitting room and dining room, each of which possessed the original long, elegant windows that had once lit the social gatherings of Regency times. The big sitting room also held the lovely marble fireplace and the tall, double doors, unchanged except for secure locks, which opened onto the landing and the grand, mahogany-bannistered staircase. The fact that the room was half its original height, part of the upstairs flat being built into the old ceiling space, did not detract from the gracious proportions of the two rooms; but that false floor was not quite as stoutly built as the rest of the house and now, carpetless and echoing, every sound was magnified. The screeching came again – the chandelier spun. Boots clattered past the double doors. Something thumped on the upstairs floor, there was the sound of scampering footsteps on the bare boards.

'It sounds as if a bloody football team's moving in!' Kate was tired. She had been working hard – too hard – and the thought of this precious, peaceful week had been all that had seen her through several fraught days. Start, she thought grimly, the way you mean to carry on. At least let them know there's a living organism underneath them and not a stone-deaf, half-witted . . . mentally spluttering she strode to the door and threw it open to find herself looking into the surprised brown eyes of the woman who stood there, hand raised to knock. For a suspended moment of shock they stared at each other, neither less disconcerted than the other.

'I say . . .' said Kate's visitor, uncertainly, 'I'm most terribly sorry, I . . .' she stopped. She was about Kate's own, average, height, with dark and somewhat untidy shoulder-length hair and wide, at this moment rather nervous brown eyes. Kate judged her to be a little older than herself – perhaps thirty-five. Under Kate's surprised eyes she lowered the fisted hand that had been raised to knock and, as if she were not sure what to do with it, she shoved it into the pocket of the thick, shapelessly shabby cardigan she was wearing. She smiled, irresolutely. 'I . . . I wondered . . . My name's Jenny Lester. I . . . that is we're . . . moving in upstairs . . .'

'Where d'yer want this, lady?' An enormous man in a leather apron, carrying a small table as if it had been a matchbox, paused on the landing as he passed.

'Er . . . oh, I'm not sure. My daughter will tell you. Just . . . just take it up . . .' she turned back to Kate, gestured a kind of helpless apology, 'I'm awfully sorry for the disruption. We're . . . well . . . a bit disorganised . . .' she spoke in short, awkward bursts, as if she had some difficulty in obtaining enough breath to sustain a whole sentence. 'I wondered . . . if I could possibly use your telephone? They . . . seem to have cut us off. Though I can't think why. I told them . . . oh, well . . .' she made a small, perplexed movement with her shoulders '. . . anyway, it isn't working. And there doesn't seem to be any electricity. Though I'm sure I told them . . .'

'Benjamin Lester, just leave that be!' a girl's voice floated down the stairwell, clear and concise. 'For goodness sake, make yourself useful for a change. Here, hold this a minute . . .'

Jenny Lester smiled her uncertain, attractive smile. 'Emily,' she said, as if the one word answered a myriad questions. 'My daughter.'

Slightly bemused – and, unaccountably considering her bad temper of a moment before, more than a little amused – Kate stepped back. 'You'd better come in. The phone's through here . . . in the dining room.'

'Thank you.' Jenny Lester followed her through the sitting room and into the dining room. Kate pointed out the phone and, politely, shut the door on her. She was poking the fire when it opened again, a little tentatively. She straightened in surprise, smiling. 'That was quick.'

'Well . . . I, er . . . actually, I haven't phoned anyone yet. I was wondering . . . do you have the number of the electricity people by any chance? I was sure I'd brought it with me . . .' she hunted again, ineffectually, through the pockets of her jeans and misshapen cardigan, '. . . but I seem to have mislaid it.'

'It'll be in the phone book, I expect. By the phone.'

'Oh. Of course. Silly me.' The other woman disappeared for a second then, sheepishly, came back into the room. 'Left my reading glasses upstairs,' she said to Kate's surprised look, 'I can't see a thing close up without them.'

Kate laughed outright. Overhead, something crashed, and Jenny winced, glancing upwards.

'I'll find it for you.' Briskly Kate flicked through the telephone directory, ran a long, manicured finger down the list of names. 'Here we are . . . Cravensford . . . that's three, two – one, nine double five.'

'Thank you.' Jenny picked up the telephone. 'Two, three . . .'

'Three, two . . .' corrected Kate.

'Of course. Three, two . . .' she dialled, stopped.

'One, nine, double five,' supplied Kate, patiently.

'Thanks.' Jenny's smile was grateful.

Kate watched her for a moment, not altogether unsympathetically. 'I'll put the kettle on,' she said.

By the time she had made a large pot of tea her new neighbour had finished with the telephone. Kate stuck her head round the dining room door. 'How many of you are there?'

Jenny looked startled, an expression that Kate, with some amusement, was beginning to think was her customary one. 'I . . . er . . .'

'For tea.' Kate relieved her confusion.

'Oh! How kind . . . Er . . . three. No . . . five, with the removal men.'

'I'll lay a tray.'

'Well, that's really most awfully kind of you. I didn't mean to impose . . .' the other woman trailed behind her across the hall and into the spacious kitchen.

'No imposition,' Kate said, cheerfully. Oddly, faced with Jenny Lester's daunting inefficiency and irresolution her ill temper, perversely, seemed to have left her. There was something in the other woman's candid brown gaze that she liked very much, and Jenny's uncertainty and obvious lack of confidence – normally not qualities that Kate admired in the least – touched a strange little chord of almost protective sympathy. Deftly Kate stacked cups and saucers, a jug of milk and a sugar bowl onto a tray, then fitted the big china teapot that she so rarely had the occasion to use into the last remaining space. 'There.'

Jenny eyed the tray doubtfully, smiled a little

worriedly, and made to pick it up. Kate, seeing suddenly half her stock of cups and saucers smashed to smithereens on the stairs, hastily changed her mind. 'Tell you what . . . you take the teapot, on that little tray, see? And I'll bring the rest.'

The upstairs flat was in chaos. The removal men were trying to manoeuvre a large Victorian dining table through a rather narrow door, watched with fascination by a small boy whose wide, innocent brown eyes and softly pretty face proclaimed him immediately Jenny's son. The operation was being briskly directed by a tall, slim girl with a mop of fair hair. 'Up a bit, or you'll catch the handle. That's it . . . nearly there . . .' she turned round as her mother came in behind her, and seeing Kate gave her a wide, friendly smile that lit her face to real beauty. 'Hello.' She had the bluest eyes that Kate had ever seen and absolutely nothing of her mother's shy irresolution.

'Hi.' Kate set the tray on a small table.

'This is Emily,' Jenny said, a little distractedly, her eyes on the removal men and the table, 'and that's Ben,' she waved a hand in the direction of the small boy, who looked at Kate, doubtfully unsmiling.

Emily held out her hand with another unguardedly friendly smile. 'How do you do? Who are you? Apart from our fairy godmother, that is?' she nodded her head in the direction of the tea tray.

Kate grinned. 'Kate Richards. I live in the flat downstairs. I thought you might like a cuppa?'

'Marvellous. Thanks. We're all gasping. Wait a minute . . . we've got some biscuits somewhere.'

Emily searched with her eyes, noted a large tea chest nearby, pounced purposefully upon it, and extracted, with the air of a magician, a box of biscuits. 'Here we are.'

The dining table, reluctantly, had allowed itself to be persuaded into the large living-dining room. The removal men dusted their hands and eyed the teapot approvingly. Kate, not sure of the etiquette of the occasion, waited politely to see if Jenny were going to pour the tea, but when the other woman made no move, poured it herself.

Jenny looked anxiously around. 'Is there anything else left to come up?'

One of the men drank the scalding tea back as if it had been a glass of cold water, and put the cup down, invitingly near the teapot. 'Just the beds, Mrs Lester.'

'Oh . . . of course . . . the beds. I forgot about them . . .'

Emily giggled. 'Oh, Mum!'

Her mother smiled vaguely and sipped her tea.

Emily caught Kate's eye and giggled again. 'She's awful!' she said, frankly. 'Dad always says she couldn't organise herself out of a paper bag.'

'Emily!' remonstrated her mother, mildly.

'Well, he does . . .'

Her mother's pretty face did not fall easily into stern lines. She smiled the first easy, unforced smile that Kate had seen. 'And he's right, of course,' she slipped an arm about her tall daughter's slim waist. 'Where would I be without you, my poppet?'

'Still in a paper bag?' The silly joke made mother and daughter laugh in the same second and Kate, outsider that she was, sensed the enormously strong bond of affection and humour that united these two. Another pang of pain – old, savagely pointless pain. Why hadn't they had a child, she and Stephen? How had they allowed themselves to become so totally self-absorbed that the thought of another soul sharing their lives had been almost unbearable? Next year, they had said, and then again, next year – for how many years? And then Stephen had been killed and the unthinkable had happened – there had been no more next years. She might have had a daughter – Stephen's daughter – like this, to love and to laugh with. To share her grief with. Or a son, like Ben, who stood watching her now, solemn curiosity in his face. 'I'm sorry . . . ?' she said abstractedly, for Jenny was halfway through a sentence, not a word of which she had heard.

'. . . I was saying that Jaimie – my husband – is in the Middle East. He's in oil.'

'Mum, you make him sound like some sort of Sheikh. Or a sardine.' Emily giggled again, infectiously.

Her mother wrinkled her nose at her, continued to speak to Kate. 'He designs things. Pipes and things. Something like that. For oil installations. There was a rush job – something went wrong – I never did quite work out what it was – and he had to leave at short notice. It left me to cope with the move on my own. Bit of a disaster, actually,' she added with rueful and disarming honesty.

'Don't be silly, Mum. You did ever so well,' Emily said loyally, and then added ingenuously, somewhat spoiling the effect, 'When's the electricity going on?' The winter afternoon was darkening already. The apartment was cold.

'They said they'd be round straight away.'

'And that,' the practical Kate put in, 'could mean any time in the next three hours. Do you have any wood for the fire?'

Jenny shook her head.

'I've got plenty, in the store behind the old stables. Emily, why don't you pop a coat on, and we'll go and get some?'

'Oh . . . but we couldn't . . .' Jenny began.

'Nonsense. Of course you can. You'll freeze otherwise – the central heating's controlled by the electric pump, so you can't turn it on yet. If you can get the fire going you'll have light as well as heat, and feel much more at home. Oh . . . and I've a little paraffin lamp you can borrow, if you need it. Come on Emily, let's go and find some logs . . .'

Later that evening, to her own surprise, she found herself knocking at the Lesters' door to check that the little family were safe and settled. Sheldon Hall was divided into six separate apartments, the coach house behind the house being another, and though, having lived here for five years, since the conversion had first been completed, she knew all her neighbours by sight and accorded them, as they did her, a civil 'Good morning', an occasional friendly word and an invariable and impersonal Christmas card, she had never felt the need for – had indeed actively discouraged – anything resembling a closer relationship. But something about Jenny Lester and her two children had crept in through an unsuspected chink in her usual armour of self-sufficiency. Jenny's almost childlike naivety and incompetence seemed to have brought out in her a kind of exasperated protectiveness that she had, with amusement, noticed – even on such short acquaintance – was at times virtually mirrored in Jenny's daughter, Emily. Jenny's warmly expressed and obviously genuinely heartfelt gratitude and pleasure when Kate had not only supplied the fuel for, but laid and lit the big open fire in the living room had been oddly satisfying to a Kate who usually eschewed such human weaknesses.

Emily opened the door now, smiling widely. 'Hello . . . Come in. We're having toast round your fire. I was quite sorry when the electricity came on!'

Kate hesitated in the doorway of the big, warmly welcoming room. Even through the immediate chaos of moving, an attractively homely atmosphere pervaded the room. Two comfortable old settees had been pulled close to the roaring fire, a small table between them spread haphazardly with plates, knives, cups, an open jar of marmalade and butter, still in its paper, on a plate. Ben sat on a thick rug in front of the fire toasting bread on a long brass toasting fork, an entrancing look of concentration on his small face. Jenny was curled up on one of the settees, her jeaned legs tucked beneath her, an open book and her glasses discarded beside her, watching him. Small shaded lamps threw pools of light around the tableau. The look on Jenny's face as she turned and caught sight of Kate standing like a statue in the shadows of the doorway was pure friendly delight. She held out a hand in a most natural way, as if welcoming an old friend.

'Kate! How nice! Come and have some of Ben's marvellous toast. It's much better than the toaster makes. He's the expert. Isn't he clever? Takes after his father, I guess – technically minded!' She laughed happily. The family safely ensconced in warmth and what looked like habitual untidiness, the worried look had left her face.

For one moment Kate hesitated, tempted to make an excuse, to leave this unlikely and unlooked-for friendship before it developed. Before it demanded something of her that she might not be ready, or prepared, to give. Tempted to leave this close-knit, happy little group to their own devices and retreat to the safety of her silent privacy.

'You can have crumpets if you'd prefer,' Emily said, solicitously, clearing an armchair of a pile of books and papers and dumping them unceremoniously on the floor. 'Though they are a bit indigestible, done by the fire. And Ben's not so good with them. He burns the edges a bit.'

'I do not!' said Ben, in peaceable, automatic contradiction, without looking up.

Kate smiled and moved into the fire- and lamp-lit circle. 'Toast would be fine. Thank you,' she said.

CHAPTER TWO

The week that followed the upheaval of the Lesters' arrival at Sheldon Hall was an astonishment to Kate. After the car crash that had killed Stephen three years before she had withdrawn to a stronghold of books, of music and of jealously guarded memories. She had – very successfully – made her work her purpose in life, had drawn back almost unconsciously from human warmth and companionship. In a world without Stephen such things seemed to have become worthless, and she had not wanted them. Yet in some strange way the intrusion into this private world of Jenny Lester and her children had breached the wall she had so carefully constructed about herself and, no matter how hard she might try to ignore that breach, it affected her profoundly.

A couple of days after their arrival Jenny called shyly at Kate's door with a large bunch of flowers – a combination, she said, of thank you present and apology.

'Thank you for what? Apology for what?'

'Kate, dear, don't be silly. I really don't know what we would have done without you these past few days. I'd never have got the place even half way straight without your help. You may have noticed . . . I'm not the best organised person in the world . . .'

Kate smiled at that. 'You really don't have to thank me. I've enjoyed it.'

'And then . . . your holiday . . . we've disrupted it so . . .'

'Don't be daft. I told you . . . I've enjoyed it . . .' Kate took the flowers, stepped back from the door. 'Do come in. I'll put these in water. They're lovely. Thank you.'

Jenny followed her into the kitchen, stood watching as Kate took a vase from the cupboard and ran water into it. 'You're back at work on Monday?'

'That's right. Nose to the grindstone again. There's a meeting I have to attend first thing Monday morning.'

'I think it's fantastic. Company Secretary. I don't think I've ever known a lady Company Secretary before.'

Kate grinned. 'No one else in the place can add up, that's all. Now – how about a cuppa?'

It was the first of many such visits. Imperceptibly, and with no sudden or dramatic turn, Kate's life changed. She spent the occasional evening with Jenny. Emily took to wandering in and out of Kate's flat at all hours of the day despite her mother's often-expressed concern about Kate's privacy. To Kate's own surprise she found in fact that she did not mind in the least. In no time she and Emily had laid the foundations of a fast friendship. Flattered by something she recognised to be close to hero-worship in the younger girl, Kate had also discovered a depth in Emily that intrigued and to a certain extent surprised her. She reminded Kate strongly of her own youth, its delights and its fervour. The girl's nature was passionate, her brain keen. She was, in some ways, more mature than her mother and more intuitive, whilst retaining an unspoiled artlessness that charmed Kate. While Jenny had won Kate's heart with her ingenuous warmth and scatterbrained impracticality, it was with Jen's daughter that she found herself spending most of her time – talking, reminiscing, discussing and explaining things she had thought were locked in silence for ever. It was with some amusement that she reflected, a very short time after their first meeting, that the girl probably knew as much about her as did anyone else living in the world. It was easy to confide in this bright, eager youngster, half-child, half-woman, wholly committed to friendship. On the drearily cold day that she arrived home from work to find the sitting room fire ready lit, her favourite Beethoven on the turntable of the hi-fi and a pot of soup bubbling on the hotplate in the kitchen, their intimacy was sealed.

'Emily . . . you shouldn't have gone to all this trouble!'

'Why not? I enjoyed it. Can I stay and talk to you while you eat your soup? Or would you rather have it in peace?'

'Stay. I'd like you to. Oh . . . by the way . . .' in the act of taking off her coat, Kate paused, 'I found those other old photos I was telling you about. They're in the cupboard there. Would you like to see them?'

On Saturday afternoon, with Jenny and Ben shopping in Cravensford, Emily took very little persuading to stay behind and spend the afternoon with Kate.

'You know a tremendous lot about the house, don't you?' She was standing by the tall window of Kate's sitting room, looking out over a countryside darkened by leaden, snow-laden clouds that lay upon the treetops like blankets of darkness. 'How did you find it all out?'

Kate stirred the embers of the fire and wedged another log into the grate. 'Well, as I told you, Stephen and I grew up in Sheldon, on the Garfield Estate. We lived two doors away from each other, in Preston Street. I can't remember a time when we didn't spend every spare minute together. We went to the same school. Part of the grounds of the Hall were used as playing fields in those days. The house was shut up, of course, and we weren't supposed to come here. But it didn't stop us. There was something about the place that fascinated both of us . . .' she paused, staring thoughtfully into the flames. Emily stood very still, watching her. 'There was an old caretaker at that time, before the house was completely abandoned. We made friends with him. He'd worked all his life for the family – the Descarts – who lived here for generations, until they had to leave, after the Second World War. He loved the old place – knew all the stories and the history. It was he who told us about the Royalist Descart, Rupert, and the tree by the lake, that I mentioned the other day.' She picked up the brass poker and tinkered with the log, sending sparks flying. 'Stephen made up a wonderful game based on that story, I remember.' She was silent for a moment before resuming, 'The old man used to let us come into the house. You can't imagine how we felt about it – as if it were ours – our secret place. Oh . . .' she shrugged, 'I suppose, looking back, other kids must have come here too, but I never remember seeing them. Noticing them.' As we never noticed anyone when we were together. She did not voice the thought. 'There were odd pieces of furniture left in some of the rooms. We used to pretend that we lived here – used, almost I think, to believe that we did. Or perhaps that we had, in another time, another life. When the old man left and the place was left empty we used to spend every spare minute here, winter or summer. It was like another world. It was another world.' She glanced to where Emily stood listening. 'Do you know the Garfield Estate?'

Emily shook her head.

'Dreary little 'thirties houses with back gardens like strips of dirty ribbon and rooms you couldn't swing a cat in. No wonder we loved this place.' She paused for a long, pensive moment. 'We went to the local library – found out quite a lot there. As a matter of fact, Stephen once did a project on the Hall. As part of something he was doing at school. Drawings, essays, that sort of thing. I can't lay my hands on it right this minute, but I could look it out if you were interested?'

'Yes, please.' Emily's voice left no doubt as to the degree of her interest. She left her contemplation of the bleak countryside, came to the warmth of the fire and knelt beside Kate, her arm across Kate's knees. 'Kate?'

'Mm?'

'Have you kept absolutely everything of Stephen's?'

'Yes.'

'Doesn't it . . . hurt sometimes?' The brilliant eyes flicked up from under long, saffron lashes, as if the girl were afraid of perhaps having trespassed too far.

'Of course.' For the umpteenth time Kate wondered why she did not resent such questions from this girl when she detested them from others. 'Sometimes. But what else would I do with them? Throw them away? That would be a lot worse.'

'Yes, I can see that.' Emily's voice was soft. 'I wish I'd known him,' she said, so quietly that Kate could barely make out the words. Emily's eyes were on the photograph on the mantlepiece. 'I'd really like to see his project on the house,' she added, more briskly, 'I love the place already. I want to know as much as he – that is as you both – did.'

'I'll hunt it out tomorrow.'

'Thanks.' Emily drew her knees up, and a little despondently rested her chin on them. 'Ugh.'

'What's up?'

'Talking of projects and things has reminded me – I'm starting that wretched new school on Monday.'

Kate touched the tangled fair hair with a gentle finger, her eyes sympathetic. 'You'll be all right. You'll enjoy it once you're there.'

'Fifteen isn't a good age for changing schools you

know.' Emily wasn't going to be convinced that easily. 'Everyone's got their friends already. I don't suppose anyone'll want me.' It was said with such determined gloom that Kate could not help laughing. Emily lifted a slightly hurt face, caught the twinkle in Kate's eye and giggled herself, her mood changing in a flash.

'I want you,' Kate said. 'You see? You've made a friend in Sheldon already.'

Emily, never one to sit still for long, jumped to her feet. 'Can we look at that old photo album again? The one with the pictures in it of the house before it was converted?'

She settled by the fireside with the book, pored over the photographs, absorbed. 'Just look at how overgrown the courtyard is. What a shame they had to cut down that lovely old tree. And gosh, look, the front door's almost off its hinges . . . and . . . Kate?' her voice was suddenly astonished, '. . . That isn't you and Stephen, is it? On horseback?'

Kate glanced at the photograph. 'Yes, it is.'

Emily turned an astonished face to her. 'But . . . the other day, when I was talking about riding . . . telling you how much I loved it . . . you didn't tell me that you rode . . . ?'

'I don't any more. I used to.'

'And very well, too, from the look of it.' Emily had taken the photograph from the book and lifted it up to the light, to see it better. 'That's no carthorse you're on there. And, Kate, how super you both look! What smashing outfits! Mix and match!'

Kate laughed, the slightest edge of strain in the

sound.

Emily glanced at her, frowning a little. 'Kate? What is it?'

Kate shrugged a little, a mute mixture of apology and self-rebuke. 'It's just . . .' she stopped. 'We had those outfits made the year we were twenty-one. The year Stephen came home from university. The year we were married. We'd always ridden together, it was one of those things we shared.' She stood up, wandered to the window. 'We used to ride from here – from the old stables. It wasn't a fashionable riding school then as it is now. It was run when we were children by a crotchety old woman called Mrs Erskine. Stephen and I used to help about the place and in return she used to let us ride the horses. It was the only thing I could do better than him.' She looked out to where the narrow drive ran between its hedged banks from the house to the big iron gates, some half a mile away, saw in her mind's eye a small girl, dark hair flying, pressing Rainstorm to the Devil's Leap, laughing as Stephen watched, afraid to follow. 'We always promised ourselves that one day we'd have proper riding outfits. The ones in the picture were our wedding presents to each other.'

'Why don't you ride now?'

With a sharp gesture Kate drew the curtains, shutting out the cold and the gathering darkness. 'I don't know – after the crash, with Stephen gone, I just couldn't somehow. I suppose it just brought back too many memories.'

'Would you ride now? With me?'

Kate shook her head. 'No. I'm sorry, Emily, truly I am. But I can't. I don't even want to try.'

Emily, her blue eyes on Kate's face, judged it time to lighten the mood. 'Mum's going to learn, did you know? She's always said she wanted to, but she's never got round to it. Now – with the stables right on her doorstep – she's got no excuse. Can you imagine? What a laugh! Knowing her, she'll forget which end of the horse is which!'

'Emily! Honestly, the way you talk about poor Jen! She isn't that bad . . .'

'I wouldn't bet money on it.' The cheerful voice came from the doorway. 'Hello, you two. Emily, love, I seem to have mislaid my key . . .'

'It's okay. I've got mine.' Emily scrambled to her feet to greet her mother with a hug. Ben, beaming, bounced into the room. 'Mum bought me some Lego . . .'

Kate smiled at Jenny. 'Stop and have a cup of tea with us? I was just going to make some.'

'Love to.'

As Kate relieved her friend of her coat she remembered Emily's words. 'Emily's just told me you're going to learn to ride?'

'Hopefully.' Jenny made a characteristic, self-deprecating gesture. 'If I don't fall off too often.'

'Look at this.' Emily thrust the photograph she had been studying into her mother's hand. 'You should get yourself an outfit like that. Doesn't Kate look stunning?'

'She certainly does. But don't be silly, darling. An

outfit like this would cost a fortune. And your poor father's had to foot quite enough bills lately. It would be terribly extravagant of me to splash out on riding clothes before I discover whether I can actually learn to ride.'

'Well, Miss Jenkins at the stables isn't going to think much of you in welly boots and an old cardy,' responded her daughter, heartlessly, 'I can tell you that.' She grinned mischievously. 'Sets quite a store by the right gear does our Miss Jenkins. Boring old bag.'

Impulsively, and without giving herself time to think, Kate caught Jenny's arm. 'Why not borrow mine? We're almost exactly the same height and build. And I never use them. It's miles more comfortable to ride in the right clothes – it might give you just the start that you need – you might as well take the lot, until you get round to buying your own . . .'

Jenny held up the photograph. 'You mean this outfit? Oh, Kate, I couldn't possibly . . .'

'Well, of course you can. Tell you what – come in to the spare room right now and I'll find them for you. You can try them on.'

Leaving a happy Ben constructing a space station on the dining room table they went in to the spare bedroom. Kate opened a wardrobe door. 'Here we are.'

Two riding outfits hung, side by side. The smaller one had a black corduroy velvet jacket and light, stone-coloured jodhpurs. The masculine outfit reversed the colours – the distinctive and beautifully cut jacket was stone-coloured, the jodhpurs black.

'I say!' With curiously gentle hands Emily drew out the man's outfit. 'Isn't that great?'

'Yes. I always used to love to see Stephen in it.' Kate's voice sounded odd in her own ears. She saw the quick look that flashed between mother and daughter. She could not help it. There were and had always been times when it seemed that Stephen hovered, somewhere, just beyond reach, times which were an agony, as if she waited for him to walk through the door, to call her name. Knowing that he would not.

'Sorry.' Awkwardly for her, Emily rammed the hanger back into the wardrobe, bright banners of embarrassment flying in her smooth cheeks. She picked up the smaller, black jacket and held it up. 'Come on, Mum. Try it on. It looks as if it were made for you. I'll bet it looks smashing . . .'

The threatened snow fell that night. Kate woke in the morning to an unmistakable, muffled stillness and a reflection of snow-light through the closed curtains. She slipped out of bed and drew the curtains. In the half-light of dawn the park lay, mantled and shrouded in a smoothly brilliant cloak of white that negated colour and shadow and made a glittering fairyland of the countryside. Later, she pulled on her wellingtons, muffled herself up in fur jacket, scarf and gloves and set out across the smooth white wasteland towards the lake. The sky was a painter's palette of pale, wintry colour, rimed with gold from the low-slanting sun. Her feet crunched through the icy crust and sank crisply into the virgin, calf-deep snow. She remembered the snowman that she and Stephen had built in this very field, the first winter after they had moved into Sheldon Hall, happy as children.

'Kate! Wait!'

Emily was running towards her, scarf flying, her cheeks bright with cold, her blue eyes bluer than ever in the rose of her face, her fair tangled curls escaping wildly from beneath the woolly hat that their young owner had clamped upon them. Kate stopped, smiling. Panting and laughing, Emily joined her.

'Isn't it super? Just *look* at it . . .' the girl spread her arms wide, as if to embrace the whole of the cold, beautiful world. 'Where are you going? To the lake? Can I come? If you'd rather I didn't . . . ?'

'Of course not.' They turned and tramped across the field together towards the dark fringe of trees in the near distance.

'Oh, look . . . Kate, look at the little robin! How he stands out in the snow! Gosh – I'll bet his poor little feet are cold!' Emily was fairly dancing beside her. Their breath fogged the clear air. Emily bent and scooped a handful of snow which she made into a snowball and threw as far as she could with an irrepressible burst of young energy. Kate laughed, delighted at the picture her young companion made. Suddenly and irresistibly her spirits lifted. It *was* a lovely day. A beautiful day. She began to hum softly beneath her breath as she walked.

'What's that?' Breathlessly, Emily picked up the tune and sang with her as she walked, 'De dum de dum, de dum de dum – oh, I know. It's *Barbara Allen* isn't it? We used to sing it at school.' She lifted her head and, absolutely unselfconsciously began to sing in a clear, tuneful, carrying voice. *'In Scarlet Town, where I was born . . . there was a fair maid dwelling . . .'*

Another memory. Stephen's favourite song. The only one, he used to swear, that he could carry in his not very musical head. How many times had they sung it together, tramping like this through the fields and woods? And why did it no longer hurt to hear those familiar words sung by a sweetly unfamiliar voice? She found her own voice lifting with Emily's. '*. . . Sweet William on his deathbed lay . . . For love of Barbara Allen . . .*'

Their voices rang across the empty field, the simple, bitter-sweet love story that had survived so many centuries echoing to the wide and shining sky.

'*. . . The more it tolled, the more she grieved . . . She bursted out a cryin' . . .*' Kate stopped, uncertain of the words. Emily's clear voice lifted alone, *'Oh pick me up, and carry me home – I fear that I'm a dying . . .'*

In the distance, by the lake, a figure stood, stone-still, head lifted as if listening, the silhouette shimmering darkly with the brilliance of lit water behind it and the blinding light of the snow blurring its outline. Kate narrowed her eyes against the glare.

'They buried Will in the old churchyard . . . And Barbara in the new one . . . And from William's grave grew a wild dog-rose . . . From Barbara's a sweet briar . . .'

The figure by the lake had gone, hidden perhaps by the trees. Kate steered Emily towards the gap that she knew was the lake path. '. . . *And there they tied in a true lovers' knot . . . The red rose and the briar . . .*'

In the sudden silence, a startled wood pigeon flapped noisily through the bare branches. Emily hummed again, a snatch of the simple, lilting tune. 'It's a smashing song, isn't it? Bit sad, though.'

'It was Stephen's favourite.' Kate lifted her head, listening. Above Emily's light voice and the scrunch of their footsteps, came the sound of someone whistling. *'In Scarlet Town, where I was born . . .'*

'Do you hear something?'

Emily stopped singing and listened. In the silence a bird called. Emily shook her head. 'No.'

Kate shrugged. 'There's someone by the lake. He must have heard us singing. He was whistling *Barbara Allen.*'

Emily giggled. 'Do you think we'll be had up for disturbing the peace?' and, without waiting for a reply, 'Oh Kate – darling Kate – I'm so glad we moved here. I didn't want to come at first, with moving schools and all that – but oh, it's such a lovely place to live! And we've found you, too.' She turned her head to look into Kate's face. 'You don't mind, do you? Us, I mean – coming and wrecking your peace and quiet?'

'No, I don't mind. Far from it in fact.' The words were a simple statement of fact. Icicles hung from the bare, spreading branches of the trees, glittering drops of water dripping from them like diamonds in the weak warmth of the winter sun. In just such a way, Kate realised, something within her was melting; that cold core of misery that she had nurtured so stubbornly over the past three years. Nothing, absolutely nothing, could ever ease entirely the pain of Stephen's loss. Nothing and nobody would ever take his place. But she was alive. And the world, lit by her young companion's laughter, was as beautiful as she had ever seen it.

From the direction of the shimmering lake came a softly-echoing sound – a few whistled bars of the song they had been singing, mingled with a sudden, sighing movement in the branches of the trees as a small, chill breath of winter air stirred the woodlands and sent little flurries of snow drifting through the treetops. Something hit Kate on the shoulder, making her jump. She turned. Emily, in the act of throwing another snowball, retreated, laughing, behind a tree. Swiftly Kate scooped up a handful of snow and started towards her purposefully, to be hit by a well-aimed snowball before her own could find its mark. Shrieking with delight, Emily took to her heels and fled through the woodland, her breath caught between helpless laughter and the effort of running. Like children they dashed, whooping, through the trees and down to the deserted lakeside, where they leaned, panting and laughing still, against the trunk of a fallen tree, brushing the powdery snow from their clothes and trying to regain their breath. As their thumping hearts quieted and the healthy glow of excercise warmed their faces and hands they stood looking over the half-frozen water to the delicate tracery of frost that patterned the brambles and reeds along the banks. In silence they stood, and in silence the lake lay like untouched silver in the glacial light.

'Did you ever see anything so lovely?' Emily asked, her voice low.

Kate turned her head and studied the bright, earnest face with its elf-locks of golden hair. 'No,' she said, sincerely.

They strolled back to the house with the chill beginning to bite at toes and fingers and an ominous edge of cloud building up to the east. 'Looks as if it'll snow again,' Emily said. 'Why don't you come upstairs this afternoon? Mum's got some chestnuts. We're going to roast them in front of the fire.'

'Sounds lovely. If you think Jen wouldn't mind.'

''Course she wouldn't. She loves to see you.' Emily swiped, idly destructive, at the tall, snowy grass with a switch of hazelwood that she had picked up. 'She's very lonely, you know. She misses Dad badly.' A few more steps. 'So do I.'

Kate glanced at her. A shadow flickered in the expressive eyes. Kate held out her hand and with a quick acknowledging smile the girl took it.

'Do you know when he'll be back?'

Emily shook her head. 'Months, he said. The summer perhaps. We don't know.'

'At least he is coming back.' The words were out before Emily could prevent them. She nibbled her lip.

'Oh, Kate – darling Kate – I'm sorry. How stupidly clumsy of me.' There was real distress in the brilliant, forget-me-not eyes.

Kate shook her head. 'No, don't be silly. And don't be sorry. The past is past. I'm only just beginning to realise that myself. And the future . . .' she glanced sideways at Emily's worried face, 'Well, just for the moment, the future's roasted chestnuts. What could possibly be better?' and smiled, at the reward of Emily's laughter.

CHAPTER THREE

'Look, Kate.' Ben, perched a little precariously on the barrel back of a small brown pony grinned from ear to ear. 'I'm a cowboy.'

'You'll be a cowboy with a broken leg if you don't watch out,' retorted his sister tartly. She was mounted on a lovely little bay, her slim back straight as an arrow, her blonde curls stuffed, haphazardly as ever, into her riding hat. Her young hands looked strong and confident on the reins. Kate felt a pang of regret for something irrevocably lost; and lost it was, she knew that beyond doubt. Had proved it.

The bay danced sideways, and Emily controlled it expertly, leaning forward to stroke the arched neck, clicking her tongue softly and reassuringly. The animal calmed. Emily looked at Kate. 'Kate . . . won't you come with us? I do wish you would. Perhaps . . . if you tried . . . ?'

Kate shook her head, smiling. She had confided to no one about her one recent attempt to overcome her strange aversion to riding, which she had once so loved. A week or so before, whilst watching one of Jen's lessons this same sense of loss had suddenly overwhelmed her and, as her friend had inexpertly and slightly nervously perambulated around the sanded ring upon an elderly, sedate mare she had determined to make an effort to get back into the saddle herself. She had deliberately not gone to the Sheldon Hall stables, but had visited a riding establishment on the other side of Cravensford. The horse had been led to her – a little, docile grey with dappled flanks and a white mane. Her foot had never reached the stirrup. With the smell of the animal, and of its polished leather accoutrements had come a wave of intolerable memories bringing with them a pain that had verged on nausea. No, this was the one thing that it appeared that she could not yet overcome. This was Stephen's, and her ability and inclination to ride had apparently died with him, perhaps for ever. 'No,' she said now, 'I can't, Emily. It's best left. Truly.'

Emily looked down at her with that shadowed sorrow in her eyes that Kate had seen before, when the thought of Stephen was there between them, and which was part of a sensitivity beyond the girl's actual years. Kate patted the bay's neck, smiling up at the slim figure above her that was silhouetted against the bright spring sky. 'It's all right, Emily.'

The lovely, earnest face was grave for a moment longer, then Emily smiled to rival the brilliant sunshine and once again Kate marvelled at the wordless communication that had been established between herself and this young, golden stranger.

'Where's Mum?' asked Ben. 'She's late again.' His voice expressed no great surprise.

Miss Jenkins had joined the group. She rode a

handsome, strong-looking chestnut horse with ease and confidence. 'Good morning, Mrs Richards. Is Mrs Lester not joining us after all?'

'Oh yes. I'm sure she is. But she hasn't come down yet.'

Miss Jenkins made a small noise with her tongue and looked down, pointedly, at her watch.

'I'll go and get her,' said Kate.

She turned and slipped back through the small door at the back of the house. When she reached the wide front hall she stopped. Jenny was coming down the stairs at a run. Her jacket – or, more accurately Kate's jacket – was undone, her hair had already escaped the restraint of the ribbon she had tied around it, and she carried her riding hat and crop in her hand. As she swung, breathless, around the mahogany newel post and saw Kate she made a small, helplessly exasperated gesture that encompassed a range of emotions from self-derision to a kind of half-amused despair.

'Oh, Kate – I honestly think I've got a screw loose this morning! Looser than usual, I mean. I couldn't find anything – just anything! – and then I left the kettle on and the damned silly thing blew up on me, and I'd deadlocked the door and couldn't find the key, so I couldn't get out, would you believe . . . ! And . . .' she had dropped her hat and crop onto the stairs and was frantically buttoning her jacket.

Kate laughed. 'You've got your buttons and button-holes mixed up. Calm down. Here . . . let me . . .' she stepped forward, unbuttoned the lop-sided jacket and buttoned it up straight.

Jenny fiddled distractedly with her hair. 'I suppose the dreadful Miss Jenkins is waiting for me out there with that expression on her face? Honestly, Kate, she terrifies me, d'you know that? *Terrifies* me . . .' she jammed her hat onto her head, '. . . even more than the damned horses do. And that's saying something.' She pulled a face, half comic, but there was a noticeable flicker of nervousness in her eyes. 'Do you think I'm quite ready for this? I mean . . . I've never been outside of that nice, safe, sandy ring before. I'm not at all certain that . . .'

'Nonsense. You've come on marvellously in these past few weeks. Miss Jenkins wouldn't be taking you out into the park if she didn't think you were perfectly competent, now would she?'

'I suppose not.' Jenny sounded far from convinced. 'Where's that damned crop?'

'On the stairs. And Snowy's a wonderfully docile animal.'

'You can say that again. In fact if she were any more docile she'd be asleep most of the time,' said poor Jen, gloomily. 'Neither of us is exactly Grand National material, would you say? Snowy's as dumb as I am. Ben's pony's got more life in her. But then,' she added, characteristically candid, 'Ben's already a better rider than I am. I'm beginning to think this whole idea wasn't such a good one after all. I'd give it up, except that I told Jaimie in my letters that I was learning, and he seemed keen, so I'm determined to do it. I'm always starting things and not finishing them. How do I look?'

'As a matter of fact, you look terrific.' Kate, smiling, surveyed the trim figure in the flattering, close-fitting jacket and well-cut jodhpurs. 'Really you do. Terrific, but a bit panic-stricken,' she added with friendly honesty. 'Now don't worry. You'll enjoy it.'

Jenny regarded her with doubtful brown eyes. 'Whenever people say that,' she said, 'I want to run a mile. My mother once said it about the dentist.'

Kate walked back with her out into the April air. It was early in the month and one of the first truly springlike days after a very cold winter. There was real warmth in the sunshine. A blaze of daffodils spread beneath the trees which shaded the stable block, their colour a pure, brilliant gold in the sunlight. Jenny, under the coolly repressive eye of Miss Jenkins, scrambled inelegantly but safely into the saddle. Snowy, to her credit, stood like a rock.

'That's it, Mrs Lester. Back straight, elbows and knees in . . . watch your hands, Emily . . . right . . . off we go . . .' Miss Jenkins led her little cavalcade at an ambling walk across the gravelled courtyard. Jenny caught Kate's eyes, rolled her own to heaven and – clinging grimly to the reins and looking a little as if she were riding to her own execution – set off uncertainly after her. Ben bounced happily behind on the small, fat pony. Emily raised a hand in farewell and brought up the rear, the little bay tossing her head, anxious to be away. Kate watched them pace beneath the trees and turn out of sight around the corner of the stable block. Emily's voice floated to her, clear and happy, and she heard Jenny's laughter. Then the sound of hoof and clinking harness faded and she was left alone. She lifted her face to the sun. It was Saturday, and after a hard week she had the day to herself. She might go for a walk. She loved the woods at this time of the year.

'Good morning, Mrs Richards.' A young woman with a baby perched on her crooked arm smiled cheerfully as she passed. She lived in one of the ground floor apartments, had lived there for nearly three years. It was with something of a shock that Kate realised that she did not know her name.

''Morning,' she said, smiling.

'Lovely day.'

'Yes. Lovely.' Thoughtfully Kate walked back into the cool shadows of the house, the little, insignificant incident triggering a train of thought in her mind that had lately recurred rather frequently. More and more over these past few weeks she had come to see that her life in the past few years had been as enclosed and self-centred as any hermit's. She had, perforce, lived in the world, but in no way had she been a part of it. She had allowed her hurt, her desperate sense of loss, to cut her off from the people around her. She had lived with a ghost whose presence had blinded her to everything else. At first, for instance, after Stephen's death, her colleagues at work had made honest and solicitous attempts to include her in the social outings, the drinks at the pub, the communal lunches that were occasionally arranged. She had been invited too to people's homes – to dinners, and to parties. And every invitation she had unfailingly – almost unthinkingly –

refused. Now, she had recently realised with something of a jolt, these invitations had stopped altogether. People simply weren't interested in banging their heads against a brick wall. Musing, she started up the stairs. Saturday. Shouldn't she, perhaps be looking forward to doing something on a Saturday night? Suddenly, cheese on toast and the television did not have quite the appeal that it might. It would have been nice, she found herself thinking, just once . . . to get dressed up . . . to talk to someone . . . The idea struck her like a ray of sunshine. A dinner party. She would have a dinner party, with Jen, and Emily – and Ben too if he could stay awake. If not, he could sleep in the spare room until the others went back upstairs. They'd have wine, and candles on the table – her steps quickened and she ran up the last few stairs to the big double doors of her flat – and she would, yes she would, dress up a little. And perhaps – in a couple of weeks' time, she'd have a real dinner party. She'd ask Natalie, from work, and her husband – what was his name? – David. And perhaps Mr Brown and that nice little wife of his who unfailingly sent a concerned little note in her Christmas card each year. Hardly a gathering to be reported in the *Tatler* – but a start. Humming to herself she unlocked the door and then pushed it to behind her. The big sitting room looked delightful; sunshine streamed through the window and lay in a bright pool across the floor, a vase of daffodils on the mantlepiece lit the room with their colour. She adjusted one of the flowers and their sweet, springlike scent filled the air. From his silver frame Stephen watched her, half-smiling. She picked up the frame and looked into those enigmatic dark eyes for a long, long time. Stephen. My love. My childhood friend. Lover. Husband. How much I've loved you. How much I love you still. But Stephen, I'm alive. Now. And I have to live. I'm here, and it's spring . . . She lifted her eyes to the mirror above the empty fireplace and for the first time in a very long time actually looked at her own reflection. Oh, to be sure, she saw it every day when she brushed her hair, or put on her makeup; but now, with deliberation, she studied the face that looked back at her. Unsmiling, it was a little severe, the dark, winged brows too positive and the sharply defined bones too strong. Yet her dark hair still shone, and her eyes, that Stephen had always called woodland violet, were tolerably attractive. Pensively she put a long finger to the faint lines that creased the corners of her eyes. She had always had them. Laughter lines, Stephen had said. No wonder they were no deeper now than they had been . . .

Behind her, totally unexpectedly, a man cleared his throat and there was a flash of movement in the mirror. In her shock she nearly dropped the photograph she still held, onto the marble hearth. Heart pounding she caught it, clutching it to her breast, and spun round.

'I'm sorry,' he said, 'I didn't mean to frighten you. But the door was open . . .' he stopped, and in silence they looked at each other.

She knew who he was. His daughter was the lovely, living image of him. She had, in fact, seen his photograph, but the ill-focused image – Jenny was no more competent a photographer than she was almost anything else – had in no way prepared her for the brilliant, cornflower eyes in a face tanned honey-dark, nor for that smile, warm and lit with gaiety, that in Emily she already loved. His untidy thatch of fair hair was streakily sunbleached. He looked tired to the point of exhaustion. For an odd, suspended moment they looked at each other, he smiling, she grave. Then he put down the battered case he was carrying and extended a square, sun-browned hand.

'I'm James Lester. Jenny's husband.'

'Yes, I know.' She took the hand, very briefly, and then stepped back quickly, suddenly aware that, absurdly, she still held Stephen's picture clutched close to her body, as if to protect it. 'Emily's so like you. The relationship's unmistakable. I'm Kate Richards.'

'Yes, I know.' He smiled again at his own conscious repetition of her words, 'and I suspect that I know every bit as much about you as you do about me. Emily's letters have been full of you. And Jen's mentioned you . . . once or twice . . .'

'I'm sorry,' she said a little stiffly.

'Oh . . . please, no . . . I didn't mean . . .' he lifted a hand in consternation, 'I'm glad to have met you so soon. I've really been looking forward to it. And I'd made up my mind that one of the first things I'd do when I got back was to thank you for what you've done for them. I worried about Jen – the move, and everything – it was such damned bad luck that I should have been called away like that, just as it was all happening. I wouldn't have had it happen for the world if I could have avoided it. Jen isn't the most . . .' he paused, and grinned in a manner that was so like Emily that it was almost uncanny '. . . well, she does find it a little difficult to organise herself on occasions.'

Kate's lips twitched. 'You could say that.'

He gave a quick, amused laugh, then sobered. 'I'm sorry I startled you just now. But I went upstairs and there doesn't seem to be anyone in. I thought perhaps they might be down here with you?'

Kate shook her head. 'They're all out riding. They weren't expecting you.'

He smiled a tired smile. 'I wasn't – so to speak – expecting myself. The chance to come home came up so unexpectedly that I didn't have much chance to let Jen know. And then . . . well . . . I thought it'd be nice to surprise her.' He ran his tanned hand ruefully through his already disordered hair. 'Just at the moment I'm not so sure it was a good idea.' He squeezed his eyes shut tiredly. 'I've been travelling for the best part of thirty-six hours. I'm shattered.'

'Don't you have a key?'

He shook his head.

Kate smiled. 'Stay here until they come back. They won't be long. Sit down and rest. I'll make you a cup of coffee . . .'

He hesitated, but not for long, and his conventional protests were half-hearted. 'Are you sure you wouldn't mind?' He was already heading for the most comfortable armchair in the room, which stood by the window in the golden stream of sunshine. He subsided into it, his long legs stretched in front of him, his eyes half closed against the sun. 'God,' he said, in quiet relief, 'that's good.' He opened one eye and grinned and, once again, irresistibly, Kate was reminded of his daughter. 'There was one moment in the small hours of the morning when I began to suspect that I'd actually died and had been sent, for my sins, to a Purgatory of incessant light, movement and discomfort. I thought it very possible that I'd never be allowed to sit comfortably still again!'

She laughed. He looked, as he sprawled there, boyish and dishevelled, more like Emily's brother than her father. 'I'll get the coffee.'

Five minutes later she returned to find him sound asleep in the sunshine. Very quietly she put down the tray, watching for any sign of his waking. He did not stir. His sleep was that of utter exhaustion. The sun gilded the bones of his face, gleamed in the fair, still sweep of his lashes. His hands lay, unmoving and relaxed, on the arms of the chair. So deep was his slumber that he hardly seemed to be breathing. Kate quietly picked up her own coffee and, seating herself in the chair opposite in the deep shadows thrown by the heavy curtains, watched him sleep.

The clatter of footsteps on the stairs and the sound of Ben's childish, excited voice half an hour later bespoke the return of the riding party. Swiftly and quietly Kate ran to the door and opened it. Jen and the children were coming up the stairs. Ben was chattering, Emily was laughing, and Jen's face was positively aglow.

'Kate!' she called, when she saw her, 'you'll never guess . . . I've had the most *marvellous* time! Loved every minute of it. I couldn't believe it . . . !'

'Snowy actually galloped,' Emily said in mock amazement, then dissolved into laughter, 'Well, lumbered is more like it, actually . . .' her voice died at Kate's raised, conspiratorial finger. 'What is it?'

Kate crooked the finger, inviting them into the room, then laid it on her lips, enjoining silence. Three surprised pairs of eyes regarded her, then obediently the Lesters crept into the sitting room. Kate stood back and watched them. She afterwards thought that she had never seen such a transformation as happened in Jenny Lester's face when she saw the sleeping man in the armchair. The bemused, half laughing puzzlement died and in its place bloomed an astounded delight which by some alchemy lit her face to absolute beauty. But it was Emily who moved first. James was stirring, half awake, when she threw herself upon him.

'Dad! Oh, Dad . . . what are you doing here? How did you get here? When did you arrive? How long are you staying? Oh . . . DAD . . . !' She smothered his face with kisses, her own cheeks wet with happy tears. Catapulted into consciousness by this onslaught, her father, laughing, struggled from under the rain of kisses and came to his feet, his arms about his daughter, his eyes on his wife.

'Jaimie,' she said in faint wonder.

Emily stepped back, and Jenny flew to him, clinging to him, burying her face in his shoulder. 'Jaimie! Jaimie!'

For one instant, taking her by surprise, something moved in the watching Kate, something cold and hateful, and then it died. She laughed with the others as Ben, last but by no means least, hurled himself upon his father to be hoisted into the air as if he had been a baby. A babble of voices and laughter, of happy exclamations and unanswered questions filled the room.

'I think,' said Kate, 'that I'd better go and make another cup of coffee.'

It was later, when the happy Lesters had escorted James upstairs and she was left alone in an apartment that seemed, bereft of their company, suddenly and cheerlessly empty that the implications of Jenny's husband's homecoming began to occur to Kate. She wandered restlessly about the room, picking up the cups, straightening cushions, putting Stephen's picture, which had been left on the table, back in its accustomed place. Then, with sudden and impatient movements she hunted out a thick jumper, pulled it on over her shirt, scrambled from her skirt into a pair of jeans and pushed her feet into a pair of heavy walking shoes. Outside, the fresh April breeze stirred her hair and the scents of spring were in the air. She strode very fast, hands in pockets, across the wet fields towards the lake. Tender green cloaked the woodland and the rich darkness of bluebell leaves carpeted the ground beneath the trees. The branches were alive with birds; a squirrel skittered nervously away from her and streaked up a tree, where it sat and watched her with suspicious, bright eyes, its bushy tail an incensed question mark. The lake's surface, like ruffled silk beneath the teasing fingers of the breeze, reflected the racing shadows of the fast moving, cotton-wool clouds. She leaned against the fallen tree trunk where she had stood with Emily that snowy day a few weeks before. She could hear, as clearly as if the girl had been beside her, the sweetly tuneful voice *'In Scarlet Town, where I was born . . .'* Moodily, Kate dug a long fingernail into the rotten bark of the tree. She was glad he had come home. Of course she was. Glad for Jenny. Glad too for Emily and Ben. Especially for Emily. Emily had missed her father badly. Utterly illogically, she felt the sudden sting of self-indulgent tears behind her eyes. And for herself? Half angrily she tossed the dark hair from her eyes.

One thing was certain.

It would be back to toasted cheese and the television tonight, after all.

She hunched her shoulders to her ears and, like a disgruntled child, rammed her fists into her pockets, turning from the glittering lake to the shadow-dappled woodland path. Perhaps he wouldn't be staying too long? Perhaps, even if he did, it would not change things as she feared it might? She stopped, head down, staring sightlessly at a tiny bunch of woodland violets cowering beneath their heart-shaped leaves at her feet; and with every power she possessed she fought the certainty that somehow, inexplicably, something had changed already.

CHAPTER FOUR

The false spring did not last. The day after Jaimie's unexpected arrival the heavens descended to the level of the rooftops and wept almost nonstop for a week. The rain drifted in dreary sheets across the drenched countryside, the mornings were dark as winter and the bleak evenings closed in quickly. Not once in that week did Kate find herself coming home to the cheer of a ready lit fire, or to Emily's smile, as she had lately become used to doing. The apartment was dark and empty when she arrived – dark, empty, and for the first time that she could ever recall, lonely.

On the Friday evening, however, the quiet was disturbed by a gentle tap on the door.

'Come in. It isn't locked.'

'Kate, darling.' Jenny poked an untidy head round the door, 'where have you been hiding yourself?'

'I?'

'Why, yes. We haven't seen you all week. Jaimie thinks it's his fault!'

'Well . . . I . . .'

'Listen, we thought . . . wondered if . . . you'd like to come out with us tonight? We're going to the "21" in Cravensford. It's not too fancy, but it's fun. The food's good and there's decent music to dance to. How about it?'

'Jen . . . it's really nice of you both . . . but . . . no, I couldn't. I'd be . . .' she stopped.

'Oh, don't be an idiot!' Jen's laugh was truly amused. 'We have been married nearly seventeen years, you know. And we've had a whole week to ourselves. Of course you must come. It's time you and Jaimie got to know each other properly. And anyway . . . Jaimie thought it would be a nice way to say thank you. For looking after us for him . . .'

'Honestly, Jen, sometimes you make me sound like a nursemaid.' Kate heard the slight edge in her own voice and was immediately sorry for it. 'Look . . . it's very kind of you both to think of me, but it is rather short notice . . .'

'Rubbish. What else will you do? Go dancing with Paul Newman?' Jenny asked composedly with one of those characteristic and disconcerting flashes of outspokenness that had floored Kate more than once before.

'Well, no, of course not, but . . .'

'But nothing. That settles it. You can't deny Jaimie the pleasure of going out with a gorgeous girl on each arm. He's been looking forward to it all week. You can't disappoint him.'

Kate, not without strong misgiving, surrendered as gracefully as she could. 'Well, all right then. If you're really sure?'

'Of course I'm sure. Pop up for a drink about eight before we go, okay?'

Kate, mentally, sorted through a wardrobe of smart business clothes and rejected them all out of hand. 'Fine,' she said, with sinking heart.

At ten minutes past eight, with a pile of discarded clothes covering half the floorspace of her bedroom and the whole of the bed she eyed her full-length reflection with something less than enthusiasm and attempted, unsuccessfully, to make her freshly washed hair lie smooth and tidy as it should. She had jabbed her mascara brush painfully into her eye, and her lipstick was too bright. Muttering, viciously, under her breath, words that she normally would not dream of using, she wiped it off and applied another that she liked no better. In the past couple of hours a kind of determination not to enjoy the evening had grown to a point where she had even considered phoning Jen and pleading a headache; but recollection of Jen's candid and far from stupid gaze had deterred her from that. She straightened the black dress that was the only thing she had deemed suitable for the occasion and grimaced at herself in the glass. Black was pretty appropriate, when it came down to it. It suited her mood to perfection. Why she should be in such a mood she did not choose to analyse. She only knew that the last thing in the world that she wanted to do this evening – or any other evening for that matter – was to go dining and dancing with Mr and Mrs James Lester. It would be a disaster. She knew it.

It was. She could not unbend from the moment that Jenny, smiling happily, opened the door to her. 'Kate! We were beginning to wonder where you'd got to! Oh

. . . don't you look fantastic! It's funny . . . we're almost the same colouring, and yet I just can't wear black. I wish I could,' she laughed cheerfully. 'It makes me look like a dejected crow. Or an inept witch. I don't know why. Jaimie . . . Kate's here. Pour her a drink, would you? Gin and tonic all right?' she added to Kate in the same breath. 'I forgot to get anything else in.'

Kate nodded. Jenny was dressed in green, a simple blouse and skirt that suited her well, with a wide leather belt at her waist. The skirt was smothered in fluff. She looked down at herself. 'My God, look at the state of me. I've been under Ben's bed looking for one of his slippers. Emily! Em? Do you know where the clothes brush is . . . ?'

Abandoned, Kate entered the big, L-shaped living-dining room alone. Jaimie looked up from where he stood at a small table, pouring a drink. When he smiled she knew suddenly and with devastating certainty why she had not wanted to come tonight.

'Hello,' he said.

'Hello.'

'Your drink.' He held out the glass.

She took it gingerly, avoiding contact with his fingers as if he had been plague-ridden. 'Thank you.'

'Cheers.' He lifted his glass to her.

She did not drink. 'Thank you for inviting me tonight,' she said, primly polite. 'It was very kind. You really didn't have to.'

He raised bleached, corn-coloured eyebrows. 'I don't think that for one moment it occurred to me that I did.'

She felt an uncomfortable warmth rise in her face, gulped her drink. He covered an absurdly awkward moment with easy tact. 'We're both delighted that you agreed to come. Take a pew . . . you know Jen, it'll take her at least half an hour to find her hair brush, or her shoes, or something . . .'

'Well, no it won't cleverclogs,' Jenny said from behind him, and slipped an arm about his waist. 'Here I am, and I'm ready, so there. Where's my drink?'

'On the table.' He smiled down at her. She twirled on her heel, her skirt flaring.

'Will I do?'

'Just about. Until Sophia Loren finally manages to get hold of my telephone number.'

She stuck her tongue out at him, laughing.

Kate looked miserably down into her drink. She did not want to feel like this. She didn't want to envy Jenny. She didn't want the poisonous stirrings of jealousy to flaw the first true friendship she had formed in years. And she didn't want – above all she didn't want – to wonder what it would be like to have those brilliant eyes look at her in the way they looked at Jenny, nor to miss, for the first time since Stephen's death, the sound of a man's voice, the feel of his body.

'Oh, damn!' Jenny was hunting round one of the settees, pushing her hand down between the heavy feather cushions.

'What is it?' Jaimie was watching her with overt amusement.

'I've lost my bag. I know I had it. Oh, hell's bells . . .

I wouldn't be surprised if I'd left it under Ben's bed when I was looking for that wretched slipper!' She left the room at a run, skirts flying.

Jaimie regarded Kate over the rim of his glass. 'Jen tells me you have a very interesting job?'

She shrugged. 'I work for a company that supplies the big computer boys with various electronic bits and pieces. We're doing all right, despite the depression.' She could hear the cool businesslike edge to her voice. It could have been used to chip ice. She sipped her drink.

'You're Company Secretary, Jen said?'

'Yes.' She did not elaborate.

He waited for a moment. His eyes were puzzled. 'How long has your husband been dead?' he asked at last, softly and abruptly.

The question shocked her oddly, brought her head up sharply.

'I'm sorry,' he said. His face was deadly serious. 'Do you mind talking about it?'

She controlled her jumping nerves. 'No. Of course not. On the contrary. It's just that . . . one gets used to . . .' in the first genuine gesture she had made all evening she shrugged, wryly, 'most other people seem to find it embarrassing to mention it. I've rather got used to that. It's three years. He was killed in a car crash.'

'I'm sorry.'

She said nothing. There was nothing to be said. She had learned that long before.

He reached over and took the glass from her hand.

It was all she could do not to recoil from him, from that unwanted physical attraction that drew her to him like a magnet. He walked to the table and replenished her drink. 'You've made an enormous impression on Emily, you know.'

'It's mutual,' she said, sincerely.

That pleased him. He smiled. Somewhere inside herself she flinched from that smile. Fool! she raged. You're acting like a stupid schoolgirl with a crush! 'I'm sorry?' she asked composedly.

'I was saying . . . I was worried at first. About the move, and Emily. Changing schools and all that. She's a strange kid in some ways . . . so mature for her age, and yet . . . I don't know . . . so vulnerable. So . . . deep.'

'Comes of having a sensitive mother,' Jenny said from the doorway. 'Come on, you two, time to go.'

Kate struggled through the evening by the simple expedient of saying very little, very brightly. Quite early on she discovered a rather strange little handicap; she found herself, stiltedly, calling Jaimie 'James.' She absolutely could not use Jennie's diminutive.

'Please . . .' he said, laughing, half way through the evening, 'no one calls me James. Not since school. Please . . . call me Jaimie?' And from that moment on she did not call him anything, which he noticed – she saw it in the puzzled and almost hostile look in his eyes, the slight cooling of his attitude towards her. The worst punishment of the evening was dancing with him. He danced well and easily, as she had guessed that he would. The touch of his hand, the warmth of his body close to hers turned her legs to wood and froze the blood in her veins. She held herself rigidly away from him, fell over his feet, miserably wished herself a thousand miles distant. And as the evening wore on a constraint grew between the two of them. Jenny watched them both, the beginnings of a faint line of worry between her brows. They were all, in varying degrees, more than relieved when the unsuccessful evening was over. They drove back to Sheldon Hall in silence, Jenny fast asleep in the front passenger seat, and Kate said her thank yous and goodnights, politely, at her own front door. She did not invite them in for a drink.

She let herself in to the dark flat, leaned for a moment against the closed doors, her head tilted back, tiredly, resting on the ancient panelled wood. She reached into the still darkness around her. Stephen, where are you? I need you. Need your help. Where *are* you? You can't have gone? You must be here . . . somewhere?

Nothing.

She switched on a small light, kicked off her shoes, dropped her coat onto a chair. She was tired. She had a headache. Perhaps she was getting a cold? Yes. That must be it.

Ignoring the desolate tears that slid down her cheeks she plodded into the kitchen to find herself an aspirin.

To Kate's enormous relief and despite her fears, once the first impact and excitement of Jaimie's return faded a little her own relationship with Jenny and with Emily settled down almost into the old pattern; almost, but not quite. Kate no longer spent companionable evenings in the upstairs flat, though on occasion Jenny would pop down to see her in the evening. Emily, seeming suddenly to become aware of her unkind neglect of her new friend, called as often as she had before, and the old, easy intimacy was soon re-established. But for Kate now, like a penance, each expression on her young companion's face, each spark of laughter in the blue eyes, each unconscious gesture reminded her of Jaimie. His physical presence she avoided as much as she could. She castigated herself, deriding the way that every distant glimpse, every forced, uncomfortable meeting set her heart racing and stirred feelings she had truthfully believed dead. In Kate's practical mind love at first sight was the unlikely stuff of Victorian novels, never to be taken seriously. She quite simply did not believe in it. It was, therefore, inconceivable that it could have happened. Nevertheless, she was ready grimly to admit to herself that life for her would be much easier when James Lester went back to his blasted oil refinery.

James Lester, however, showed no great inclination to oblige her. Three weeks after he had come home – the end of his official leave – he went to London. The news that an excited Jenny brought downstairs on his return made Kate's heart, despite her friend's obvious happiness, sink.

'. . . he doesn't have to go back! Not for a while,

anyway. Oh . . . Kate . . . isn't it marvellous? I didn't dare hope . . .'

Emily was shuffling through some photographs that she was sorting for Kate, prior to sticking them into an album. 'Fantastic. Good old Dad. Where's he going to work?'

'They want him in the London office for a while. He can easily commute from here.'

'That is good news.' Kate's smile felt wooden. Her voice, she knew, lacked warmth.

Jenny glanced at her, thoughtfully. 'Em?'

'Yes?'

'Pop upstairs and keep an eye on Ben for me for a few minutes, would you? There's a good girl.'

'Sure.' Emily left them.

In the quiet, not looking at Jen, Kate began to gather together the photographs.

'Kate?'

Kate hesitated. 'Yes?'

'Why don't you like Jaimie?'

The blunt question took her breath away. 'I do.'

'No, you don't.' Jenny seated herself across the table, her hands folded in front of her, her face serious to the point of distress. 'I don't understand it. I expected you really to get on well together. Instead . . .' she gestured, helplessly. 'What is it? I don't understand it,' she repeated.

Kate, with great care, stacked the photographs and squared them off. Stephen leaned negligently on the marble fireplace where his picture now stood, one hand raised, an intent expression on his face. She remembered the day as if it had been yesterday. He had been lecturing her on how to take a portrait photograph, and she had taken it whilst he had still been talking – 'It isn't that I don't like James,' she said, and heard herself the totally unconvincing ring of the words, 'I just feel that . . . well . . . I don't like to intrude now that he's home . . .'

Jenny shook her head decisively. 'No. It isn't that. It's the way you are when you're with him. Kate, darling, you make it so obvious that you don't like him. You act as if you can't bear to speak to him. He's even noticed it himself . . .'

Kate looked up sharply. 'What do you mean?'

Jenny's tongue had run away with her. She flushed. 'He . . . mentioned it the other day. That you aren't . . . quite what he expected . . .'

'I see.' Kate's dark blue eyes were expressionless. 'In other words – as they say – the feeling's mutual?'

'No!' The word was too quick, and they both knew it. Jen reached across the table and covered Kate's hand with her own. 'Oh, Kate . . . please? . . . try. I'm sure if you get to know Jaimie you'll like him. Everyone does. You haven't given him a chance. Darling Kate . . . you've come to mean so much to us over the past few months. It's hateful that you and Jaimie don't get on as I'd like you to. Won't you please try? For me?'

Kate held out against the plea for long moments. She saw the beginnings of hurt in the soft brown eyes. Knowing the risk she took, knowing the pain she might be courting, she smiled. 'Of course I will.'

Jenny laughed in happy relief. 'Come up to dinner tonight. Talk to him. You'll love him, I know you will, once you get to know him.'

'Yes,' Kate said.

Jenny jumped up. 'I have to go. See you about eight tonight? It won't be anything special . . . you don't mind, do you?'

'Of course not.'

'And . . . Kate?' By the door, Jenny paused.

'Yes?'

'Do you think . . . as a starter . . . you could stop calling him James? He really does hate it. Call him Jaimie. Everyone does.'

Kate nodded. 'Jaimie,' she said.

It was the start of purgatory. Across Jenny's ardent efforts to bring them together Jaimie and Kate smiled coolly, conversed politely and played a game of deceit, the prize for which was the one desire they both apparently had in common – Jenny's happiness. But if Jenny was deceived, Kate knew beyond doubt that Jaimie was not. She saw often in his eyes a kind of detached, pensively questioning look which she immediately interpreted as critical, as if he measured her worth and found her wanting. For herself, her pure, physical need for him was sometimes an agony. She watched the way he moved, memorised with no volition the way his untidy hair fell across his forehead, the habit he had of stabbing the air with a square-cut brown forefinger to emphasise a point, and learned to school her face if not her emotions. She still avoided him as much as was reasonably possible, but as spring turned at last to golden summer and the evenings lengthened she found it more and more difficult. Jenny was, it seemed, always arranging something, and the something always had to involve her darling Kate. Kate had, willy nilly, become a member of the family. It took some time for her to realise that Emily too – perhaps unconsciously – had been drawn into the conspiracy, and when she realised that she knew, close to despair, that the battle was as good as lost.

She wandered, one warm May evening, alone to the lake. A couple with two young children were picnicking noisily by the fallen tree, so she pushed on round the lake edge to where, at the end farthest from the house, the woodland was deepest. There was a place there that she knew – that she had known for years – where she was virtually certain of being alone. It had been one of her and Stephen's favourite places when, as children, they had used to play in the abandoned park. It lay peacefully now, a tiny clearing in the slanting late sunlight, a columned green space roofed with rustling leaves through which the colour-washed blue of the sky glinted. She lay on her back in the cool, short grass, her hands behind her head, looking into that leaf-patterned blue distance, her mind a deliberate blank. She had thought herself round in weary circles. She could think no more. The birds in the deep woodland sang their evening songs and flitted busily in the tangled branches, living their blessedly uncomplicated lives. Something scurried through the undergrowth not far from her. The faint, sweet smell of bluebells mingled with the scent of crushed, damp grass and of last year's fallen leaves. The sunshine dappled her face and made rainbows in her lashes. Then from nowhere, there came the faintest of movements and a figure loomed over her, black against the light. Her eyes flew open. Jaimie stood looking down at her, unsmiling, the sunlight in his yellow hair. For a moment she thought that her heart had stopped beating altogether. Then it resumed, thumping irregularly, preventing speech. She did not move.

After a moment he hunkered down beside her, not sitting, but balanced on his heels, his elbows resting on his knees. 'Hi.' He still did not smile.

'Hello.'

'I made you jump again.'

'Yes.'

He was studying her face in the most open and disconcerting way, and it was with an effort that she held her own gaze steady.

'I followed you,' he said, his voice matter-of-fact.

That shook her. She came up onto one elbow, watching him.

'I think we ought to talk,' he said.

'What about?'

For the first time almost since she had known him he looked less than sure of himself. He lowered himself onto the ground beside her, crooked his knees, leaned his elbows on them. His foreign-looking tan was fading, and now there was a faint, unusual tinge of bright colour on his cheekbones. He picked a blade of grass, studied it, put it in his mouth.

Kate waited.

He shook his head abruptly. 'P'raps not.'

'Don't be ridiculous.' Perversely, and a little angrily now she wanted him to stay. 'You can't say something like that and then just walk away. Talk about what?' She sat up, her eyes sparking.

'Don't you know?' His face was sombre.

Silence fell.

Somewhere deep within Kate a tiny pulse of half-fearful excitement stirred, thumping distantly with her blood. They looked at each other, wordless, and in the quiet the excitement grew and blossomed first into an unbelieving happiness, and then almost immediately into terror as she suddenly understood. She turned her head away from him sharply. The life of the woodland went on around them as if nothing had changed. His square hand rested on the grass by her side. She studied it as if her life depended upon remembering the bones, the veins, the square, meticulously clipped fingernails.

'Kate,' he said.

She flinched from the gentleness in his voice. 'Yes?'

'I know why you avoid me. Why Jenny thinks you don't like me. Why you hate to be with me . . .'

She did not try to defend herself with lies. She knew that there would be no point whatsoever in denial. 'Then why in God's name don't you *help* me? Why do you let Jen – and Emily – throw us together so much?'

'Because I can't help myself. Because if I did, I'd

never see you, and I couldn't stand the thought of that. Because I want you as much as . . . more than . . . you want me. And I'm not as strong as you are. I have to see you. Hear you. Watch you. Touch you, sometimes.'

She bowed her head, shutting her eyes for a brief second, shutting out the impossible.

'I'm sorry,' he said, 'I had to say it.'

She nodded.

'What are we going to do?'

She turned on him fiercely. 'We're not going to do anything! We're not . . . going to do . . . *anything*!' But her quick movement had brought her too close to him, and she could not – physically could not – draw back. He kissed her, very, very gently and his kiss was exactly as she had imagined it, so many times. When at last he drew away from her she remained still, watching him.

'Oh, Christ!' With that characteristic gesture she knew so well he ran a distracted hand through his bright, untidy hair. 'Oh Christ!' he said again, in a kind of vicious misery.

'I doubt if He feels inclined to help us.' Kate started to get up. He put out a hand and caught her wrist.

'Don't go.'

She did not resist him, nor did she reply, but simply remained still, waiting for him to release her. When he did so she stood up, touched his bowed head for a moment with her finger, remembered with a pang of pain touching his daughter's corn-coloured curls in the selfsame way. Then she left him and walked steadily back to the house.

CHAPTER FIVE

She knew with a kind of desperate certainty that he would not leave it at that; knew it from the look on his face when she left him. At first, however, it looked as if she might be wrong as May turned to June and a spell of warm sunny weather brought a series of long hot days that turned the park into a golden landscape of summer. Kate took to working late at the office as the seemingly endless summer evenings lengthened the days. If she were not at Sheldon Hall she could not be tempted to try to see Jaimie alone. Jenny, laughing, complained of neglect, but lightheartedly. It astonished Kate, in fact, that life could apparently carry on so normally, that it had not changed around her as had her own inner world. How could people look at her and see her unchanged? Her mind and her emotions were in turmoil, and yet she smiled, held rational conversations, worked, as if nothing were amiss. She could not for her life decide whether the discovery that Jaimie shared her feelings made things easier or a hundred times worse. But one thing she did know; she had meant it when she had insisted that they must do nothing about the attraction they felt for one another, and the frustration of that sometimes woke her in the dark hours to tears. Yet, on the other hand, to know that sometimes he must think of her, sometimes, surely, feel some kind of sadness, in a strange way assuaged her own pain a little. It never occurred to her to doubt his declaration. Beyond reason, she knew that he had told her the simple truth. She avoided him as much as possible, but on those occasions when she was forced into his company she could not help experiencing a kind of treacherous excitement to know that, as they looked at one another, as they spoke polite and mostly meaningless words, smiled light, social smiles they shared a deeper bond that was their own and no other's. Then she would catch sight of Emily's clear, laughing eyes, or Jen's brown, trusting ones and the resultant surge of guilt would sober her to misery. At the worst times she considered leaving – selling the apartment and moving away. But although she tried to fool herself into believing that she was considering the thought in earnest it was never an option she could take really seriously. For to leave Sheldon Hall would not just be to leave Jaimie. It would be to leave her beloved home, her only friends and – perhaps most inconceivable of all – her memories. Where, in another setting, would Stephen be? Her passion for Jaimie had by no means overshadowed that other love; nothing, she knew, ever could. How could she ever leave the place that she felt she held in trust for those two young people who had invested it with a magic of their own? No – although there were times when she lay restless in her bed, unsleeping and unhappy, half convinced that she should leave, when the morning sun streamed through her bedroom window and the birds sang in the wide parkland she knew that she could not.

A couple of weeks into June, Ben's sixth birthday occurred. Asked what he would like to do to celebrate, he plumped immediately and with the certainty of long consideration for a picnic by the lake. Kate, as a matter of course, was included in the family arrangements, and, since the birthday fell on a Friday, arranged to leave the office a little early. She had bought Ben the fanciest electronic game she could find – a cataclysmic affair of space ships, aliens and popping explosions which did very little for her, but which the shop assistant assured her would delight any normal six year old. Nowadays, she informed Kate, the youngsters learned to handle computers before they learned the alphabet. Which seemed to Kate to be more than a pity, but she accepted a more knowledgeable view, paid the outrageous price and had the thing wrapped in bright paper.

When she got back to her apartment Emily was waiting. Kate kissed her cheek. 'Em, darling, you look lovely.' The girl was dressed in white. A broderie-anglaise embroidered Victorian petticoat – never in fact designed to see the light of day – that Jenny had bought at an antique fair did pretty service as a skirt, belted tightly at her slim waist. With it she wore a lacy, short-sleeved blouse with a tiny piecrust frill at the throat which set off her lightly-tanned fair skin and the brilliant eyes to perfection. She had tied back her unruly hair with a pink ribbon which dangled attractively down her back, and had tucked into the ribbon a couple of pale rosebuds. Delighted at Kate's open admiration she twirled unselfconsciously on the toes of her flat, ballet-dancer's pumps, and her skirts flared like the petals of a flower.

'Like it?'

'Love it. How much time do I have?'

'Mum said half an hour. Is that enough?'

'Oh, I should think so.' Kate went into the bedroom, depositing the birthday parcel and her bag on a chair, beginning to unbutton her blouse as she walked. 'A swift shower and a change is all I need.'

Emily had picked up a magazine and dropped into an armchair in the sitting room, her back against one arm, her slim legs over the other. 'Can I stay? It's chaos upstairs. Ben's being a pain.'

'He's excited, I expect. Of course you may.' In her towelling robe, Kate popped her head round the door, 'I've bought him one of those destructive electronic games. You know . . . war of the universe stuff . . . will that be all right, do you think?'

Emily rolled sisterly eyes to heaven. 'Ugh! Sounds as if he'll love it, the little beast. As long as it's got lots of bright lights and weird noises.'

'Oh, it's got that all right.'

Kate showered swiftly. Wrapped once more in her bathrobe she sped back along the hallway towards the bedroom.

Emily's fair head appeared round the door. 'Can I come and help you dress?'

Kate was amused. 'If you like.' She stood by the

mirror, dragging a comb through her wet hair. 'Fancy being a lady's maid, do you?'

'Oh, I always help Mum get dressed when she's going out. Mind you,' she added cheerfully, 'that's because she often needs it. I expect you can remember quite well on your own where you keep your undies, or your handkerchiefs and things?'

Kate grinned, rummaging in a drawer. 'Just about.'

'Tell you what . . .' Emily, who had thrown herself onto the bed, bounced up almost immediately, ' . . . why don't you let me choose what you should wear? Mum often lets me. And you've got such lovely things. Oh, Kate . . . can I . . . ?'

'Be my guest.' Kate waved a hand at the big wardrobe. 'Just make sure it's something cool and comfortable.'

Emily opened the door of the wardrobe wide. 'Well, now . . . let's see. That's pretty . . . but no, Mum's wearing green. You shouldn't both wear the same colour, should you? How about this . . . ? No, perhaps not. It's a bit yellow for this evening.' Kate, scrambling into fresh underclothes, her back to the girl, grinned privately at such unassailable logic. 'Ah . . . that's it. Absolutely perfect! There . . .'

Kate turned. Stopped. Felt every vestige of blood drain from her face. 'Where did you get that?'

Emily, who was standing proudly with, draped over her arms, a summer dress of pale pink with short sleeves and swirling skirt upon which was appliqued a pretty, summery pattern of white daisies, stared at her. 'Kate? Wh . . . whatever's wrong?' she stammered.

'Where did you get that dress?' Kate's voice had an unpleasant rasp in it. She felt physically sick.

'I . . . well . . . from the wardrobe . . .' Emily's young face was worriedly confused. 'It . . . it was just hanging in there. Look . . .' she gestured to a space in the wardrobe where the dress had obviously hung. 'Kate, what on earth's the matter?' She looked at Kate in growing distress.

Kate all but snatched the dress from her and then, at the dawning look of hurt in the blue eyes, made an effort to control herself. 'I'm sorry, Emily. It's just . . . well . . . I don't usually keep that dress in there. I don't wear it any more, you see.'

'But why ever not? It's so pretty.'

The ugly shock was subsiding. Kate took a calmer breath. 'I can't imagine how it got into that wardrobe. I must have moved it without thinking. It's usually in the cupboard in the spare room.'

Something like understanding dawned in Emily's openly transparent face. 'Oh, Kate, I'm so sorry. It's something to do with Stephen, isn't it?'

Kate nodded. 'It was the dress he liked me in best. I was wearing it on the night he was killed. We were supposed to be going out.' Waiting. Watching the time. At first exasperated, irritated that he should be late. Then the growing worry. Why hadn't he called? Reassuring herself. Don't be ridiculous. He's been kept late at the office . . . caught in a traffic jam . . . And then that peculiar foreknowledge, the dreadful sinking feeling of premonition as the police car had turned into the drive and rolled to a stop beneath her window . . . She shivered.

'Oh, gosh!' Emily looked at her, fiercely worried. 'I'm so sorry, Kate. Here . . . give it to me . . .' She took the pink dress from Kate's nerveless hands and ran out of the bedroom with it. Kate heard the spare room cupboard door open and close. She stood like stone, trying not to think.

'There!' A little flushed, but smiling determinedly, Emily was back. 'I've put it in the spare room cupboard. Don't think of it, Kate darling.' Kate smiled, a little shakily, at the fiercely protective note in the young voice. 'Look . . . wear the yellow. It's very pretty. Or . . . no . . .' She was foraging feverishly in the wardrobe. 'Here. That's it.' Triumphantly she had produced a dark blue shirt-waister with a red leather belt. 'That'll look lovely. It matches your eyes exactly.'

'The dress or the belt?' Kate asked, faintly, and was rewarded by Emily's infectious, if still slightly uncertain, giggle.

Emily held out the dress, her eyes still not entirely happy. 'Do put it on. It's nearly time to go.'

'Of course.' Kate pulled the thing over her head, buttoned it, pulled the belt tight. The strange sickness that the sight of the other dress had caused in her was subsiding. Her voice was back to normal. But her hands were ice-cold. 'There,' she said, very brightly, 'that'll do, won't it? Do you think Ben will approve?'

From the sitting room Jenny's voice called. 'Anyone there? We're nearly ready to go.'

'Coming.' Emily and Kate joined Jen, Jaimie and a

bright-eyed Ben in the sitting room. For the briefest of seconds Kate's and Jaimie's eyes met.

'Can I have my present now, Kate?' asked Ben with the perfect confidence of the much-loved very young.

The picnic was a great success. They played rounders until Jaimie got carried away and the ball was lost in the lake . . . 'Show-off,' Jenny grinned, fondly . . . and then took it in turns to annihilate Venusians and Martians, an activity at which Ben proved, to no one's surprise but Kate's, to be the greatest expert. They ate spicy cold chicken washed down with wine for the adults and orange squash for the other two. Emily, having knocked back her glass of squash as if she were dying of thirst, wrinkled her nose. 'Can't I have a glass of wine?'

'No.' Jaimie was adamant.

'Oh . . . oh. Go on. Just half a glass.'

'Well . . .'

Emily grinned, knowing she had won, and held out her glass. 'It *is* a special occasion, after all,' she said.

A little later, as the sun tipped the treetops and the smallest of breezes cooled the air Kate wandered alone to the lakeside and leaned against the fallen tree, her arms folded across her breast, her eyes on the glimmering water. A bird called, sweetly, in the woodland. Behind her, happy voices rang. 'Ben . . . come and see what I've found . . .' 'Emily! Be careful . . . don't go too close to the edge . . .'

She felt rather than heard him come up behind her. Her fingers, that had been loose on her upper arms, tightened, and she felt their pressure through the thin material of the dress. She did not turn.

'Kate. I've got to talk to you.'

She shook her head.

'Please.'

'There's nothing to talk about.'

'There's everything to talk about.'

She shook her head again, wordless.

He began to speak very rapidly, in an undertone, and she had the strong impression that the words were carefully picked, even perhaps rehearsed, though that in no way weakened the desperate sincerity of his voice. 'If we go on like this, never acknowledging what's between us, never talking about it, we'll do no one any good. If we spend just a little time together . . . trying to understand, to come to terms with it . . . we'll do no one any harm. Kate . . . please . . . meet me on Sunday evening, about this time, in our clearing . . . ?' She blinked at that. She knew where he meant, but 'our' clearing? That suggested a degree of conspiracy with which she was far from comfortable. 'Please,' he said again, before she could speak, even had she known what to say, 'I'll be there. I'll wait. Meet me. I must . . . I *must* . . . speak to you.'

Emily was running towards them, like a child, her hair, from which the ribbon had long since slipped, blowing in the evening breeze. 'Kate! Kate . . . come and see what I've found . . .'

'Kate!' His voice was urgent, a little rough. She still did not look at him, as she had not through the whole exchange. She sensed the anger in him.

'Kate! Dad! Come and see the little ducks . . . oh

they're so sweet!' Flushed and out of breath Emily caught Kate's hand and dragged her to the water's edge. 'Just look at them. Did you ever see anything so lovely?'

Right up until the last minute she did not intend to go. All day Saturday and all day Sunday she told herself that, determinedly; she would not go. Sunday evening proved to be even more beautiful than the preceding ones; Kate stood at the sitting room window and bleakly watched the sun as it blazed into the darkly silhouetted trees and turned the lake to flame. Was Jaimie there now, waiting for her? He had said he would. Had said he would wait. How long would he wait? ' . . . we'll do no one any harm . . .'

Restlessly she started to turn from the window, and as she did so a flash of movement in the park caught her eye. A rider flitted through the trees and into the darker shadows. Well, at any rate, someone was out and about. The thought, oddly, reassured her. Supposing . . . just supposing . . . that she took it into her head to stroll to the lake and back on such a lovely evening? It would certainly not be the first time. And supposing the same notion had occurred to Jaimie? Might they not have met accidentally? Would it be such a crime to meet so, to talk, blessedly uninterrupted, for a few minutes?

You're lying to yourself, she told herself savagely.

But it was too late. She was already at the door.

The evening was very still and the sunlight an almost tangible gold. She walked across the field towards the lake, telling herself still that she would stop at the fallen tree, and go no farther. Knowing that she would not. She did however, pause at the tree for a moment, lost despite herself in the beauty of the evening, but then she pushed on, into the deeper woodland. There was hardly any sound but the crackle of her own footsteps in the carpet of leaves, the rustle of her own movement. She wondered if Jaimie could hear it . . . wondered if he were in fact there. Half-hoped that he would not be. She paused at the thought, and silence fell about her. A bird skittered through the branches above her head. She was in a tangled patch of woodland, heavy with summer growth, through which the angled sun did not strike. She shivered a little in the cooler shadows and was about to push on when a sound came to her, not so much through the air as through the ground at her feet. The steady, muffled sound of a horse's hooves. She glanced around her, curiously. The slender, wreathed columns of the trees stretched away from her, darkly shaded against the woodland edge where, like a curtain of golden coins the sunshine hung, dazzling the eye. Movement made her blink against the brilliance of the light. A tall figure on a massive horse flickered across the barred light. The rider rode steadily across the line of her vision, silhouetted against the sun, now seen, now apparently vanished. She screwed her eyes up, straining to follow the rider's progress. There was something hauntingly familiar about the figure in the flickering, dancing blinding light, something that she could not quite grasp, like a memory of a familiar tune that refuses to come to voice. The hoof beats faded. The horseman appeared once more, fleetingly, at the far reaches of her vision, and her heart raced. Then he was gone; and she was left with a confused impression of something that she knew could not possibly be. There must be other riding outfits like that one? And there must . . . surely . . . be other riders who rode with that particular style . . . how many times had she laughed . . . ? 'Stephen . . . for heaven's sake sit up. You ride like a cowboy . . . you'll go to sleep in a minute . . .' She strained her ears, but could hear nothing but the violent and irregular beating of her own pulse. It could not be. Blindly she stumbled along the narrow path towards the clearing. A moment before she had half-hoped that Jaimie would not be there. Now she found herself praying with all her heart that he would be.

He was lying back on his elbows on the grass, his jeaned knees crooked before him, his eyes half closed. When she entered the clearing he scrambled to his feet and came towards her, smiling, his hands held out. 'Kate! I knew you'd come.' His voice, his stance, the clearing itself were all blessedly normal. What had she expected?

'That's more than I did, to be truthful.' Stiff-lipped, she lifted her face to his kiss and then found herself clinging to him in something more than passion. After a moment he put her gently from him.

'Kate? What's wrong? Come on, my dear . . . we're doing nothing so very terrible! You mustn't let things upset you so.'

She buried her face in his shoulder, trembling. His arms held her, unassailably, against the world for the moment at least. She lifted a wanly smiling face.

'Kate, for heaven's sake, what is it? If you're that upset . . . if you really didn't want to come . . . then?'

'No. It isn't that.'

'What then? You look as if you've seen a ghost.'

She cleared her throat. 'Nothing. It's nothing. Just that . . . I hate this kind of deception . . .'

'Of course.' Softly he kissed her, drew her down to the grass. She sat stiffly, her eyes on the shadowed woodland. 'Jaimie?'

'Yes.'

'Did you see anyone on your way here? Hear anything?'

He shook his head. 'Kate, oh, Kate, what a terrible conspirator you are! No one's followed us. No one's privy to our dark secret!' He kissed her, teasing a little. 'Not that there's much of a dark secret to be privy to! Not so very dark, anyway.'

That brought a more genuine smile. She looked at him. He lay back, his arms folded behind his head, watching her with bright eyes that were full of warmth and laughter. 'Have I discovered a little Puritan at heart? My darling Kate . . . love isn't for making people miserable, you know.'

She touched his face with her finger, suddenly calmer, recognising all at once the stress that had brought on her silly, over-emotional reaction to the incident of the horseman. There were always people riding around here on a summer's evening. Had she not been coming here – to meet her best friend's husband – would she have seen Stephen so clearly? Almost certainly not. 'Love?' she asked, softly. 'Is that what it is?'

'Yes.' All trace of laughter had left the cornflower eyes as he reached for her. 'Yes.'

He kissed her for a long, quiet time. Then he moved and she felt his hand on her breast, knew that he must feel the strength of her own reaction, the surge of physical desire that his touch triggered. She pulled away abruptly.

He watched her.

'That wasn't what we came here for.'

He raised fair eyebrows. 'Wasn't it?'

'No. To talk you said. To understand.'

He sat up, the shadow of impatience on his face. 'Do you really think that we need to talk in order to understand what's happened between us? Haven't we already said it all . . . with or without words? I love you . . . you love me . . .'

'But . . .'

'It happens to people. It's happened through no fault of our own, to us. We can't ignore it . . .'

'That's just what we do have to do.'

He was silent.

'Because of Jen,' she said.

Jaimie looked away, dragged at the short, springy grass with his fingers, his face suddenly sombre.

'We both love her,' Kate said, stonily.

'Yes.'

'Then we can't do this to her.'

'Do what to her, for God's sake? Why should she ever know?' He watched her, waiting. She could feel the strength of him, the savage frustration, feel his will holding her with no word spoken, no move made.

'We can't,' she said, stubbornly.

His lashes flickered and his mouth hardened a little. 'Then why are you here?'

'I don't know.' It was her turn to look away. 'I don't know,' she repeated.

'You're lying to yourself, Kate,' his voice was low and clear, not angry, not pleading, simply the voice of logic and of reason. 'Stop torturing yourself. God, girl, this is the twentieth century, not the nineteenth. We understand these things . . . don't we? You're taking nothing from Jen. You couldn't. I love her. I always will. There are things we share . . . will share in the future . . . that you can have no part of . . .' The words, cruel as they were, were spoken with tenderness as he willed her to understand. 'Don't you see that? But you . . . and I . . . this is now, and undeniable. I want you, I think, as much as I have ever wanted anything or anyone in my whole life. No, wait . . .' as she opened her mouth to speak, he held up a quick hand, 'Don't say anything yet. Let me finish. I want you to do something for me. To answer a question. Tell me . . . do you believe me to be the kind of man who embarks upon . . .' he pulled a funny wry face, 'affairs of the heart lightly, or every day of the week?'

She shook her head.

'Thank you for that at least. You're right. In fact,

you're the only woman apart from Jen that I've ever looked at. How can it be wrong? Do you believe that I love you?'

She hesitated for the space of a heartbeat, then nodded again.

'And you love me.'

'Yes.'

'Then, my darling idiot, don't you see that trying to make believe that the situation doesn't exist solves nothing. To pretend that we don't want to make love solves nothing. We've done it, in our imaginations, a dozen times already, haven't we?'

She flushed. 'Yes.'

'Then we're guilty, whether we like it or not, already, aren't we? If there is such a thing as guilt in this situation, which I'm not at all certain of.' He waited for a moment. 'Aren't we?' he asked again, insistently.

Kate remained silent.

He stood up, pulling her after him, gathered her to him and laid his cheek on her smooth, dark head. 'Don't worry, my Katie. I don't want to make you unhappy. It's the last thing I want. I'd never do anything to hurt you, I promise. Think about it. Know that I love you. And don't . . . please don't . . . be sad.'

They stood for a long time in the gathering shadows.

'I think,' Kate said at last, 'that I'd better be going.'

He held her for a moment longer, then released her. 'One day,' he said from the darkness, 'we'll make love. I know it. When the time is right and it happens naturally, we'll make love. And then you'll know it isn't wrong. Couldn't be wrong between us.'

His words followed her back to the house, balm to her doubts and uncertain emotions. One day. Not now, nor yet tomorrow, but one day. Well, perhaps that would do, perhaps that promise would assuage the ache, be the anodyne that would anaesthetise the pain of the thought of Jaimie in the rooms above her, living with Jen, laughing with her, making love with her, sleeping away those precious shared hours of darkness afterwards. Perhaps.

The moment she let herself into the flat she knew there to be something wrong with the room. She switched on a lamp and looked about her, frowning. For a moment nothing struck her as too much out of place; and then she saw it and stood, puzzled. The big armchair that had always been Stephen's and which she had moved, a couple of years ago, to a position by the window from which she could see across the park, had been shifted. It stood now, as it had used to, on the far side of the fireplace, next to a small table upon which stood a large onyx ashtray. She shrugged a little, nonplussed. Perhaps she had moved it herself, unthinkingly, that morning whilst she had been hoovering, and forgotten to put it back? There could be no doubt that her mind had not exactly been on what she had been doing. But the ashtray . . . ? Still puzzled she walked to it and picked it up. It was the one that Stephen had always used when he smoked his pipe, and since his death, as she did not smoke, it had remained unused, except by visitors, on the sideboard. What was it doing now, here, on the table beside the chair as if . . . she felt an odd sensation upon her cold skin . . . as if it were ready for use? With sudden, forcefully brisk movements she dragged the chair back into its rightful place and slammed the ashtray back onto the sideboard. A small transistor radio stood next to it. On impulse she switched it on, turning it up full blast. It was ready-tuned to Radio Three. The measured strains of Haydn filled the shadowed room. Determinedly and unusually off-key she sang along with it . . . 'De dum de dum de . . .' She left the room, switching on all the lights as she went, and walked into the bedroom, kicking off her shoes, starting to unbutton her blouse. A good strong gin and tonic was what was called for. 'Dum de dum de . . .' Then a warm bath, perhaps, and . . .

She froze.

Nothing that had gone before had prepared her for the hammer stroke of her heart. Now she saw what else had been wrong in the sitting room.

Stephen's picture had no longer been on the mantlepiece.

It couldn't have been, for it was here – on her bedside table, beside the lamp, and from the silver frame he watched her with that faint, enigmatic smile she knew so well. Very, very slowly she walked to it, picked it up, had to steady one hand with the other, she was shaking so.

What was it he said once, so long ago, as a child here in this very room, before its transformation? The words came back to her as clearly as if he were truly standing beside her. 'Silly Kate. As if I'd really leave you here alone. As if I'd leave you anywhere alone. Ever.'

In the sitting room the last, over-loud notes of the symphony orchestra faded, and in the ensuing silence in the vast darkness of the park, faintly heard, an owl hooted.

CHAPTER SIX

Her nerves were taut to breaking point. She jumped at every noise, examined every circumstance, slept badly and ate worse. Twice more in the following week Stephen's photograph in its silver frame found its way inexplicably onto her bedside table, once his worn slippers appeared beside the hearth and a couple of times, on coming home from work, she could have sworn that there was the faint smell of his pipe smoke in the air. She spent long nights reading in the lit bedroom, and most evenings was to be found wandering the grounds until darkness drove her indoors. On a day of summer rain – for, inevitably, the golden June weather had broken, and the English summer reverted to normal, she was walking through the park when, distantly, she heard the sound of children's voices. She stood for a moment, her face lifted to the rain, then she walked towards the sound. In the corner of the park a great oak tree stood, gnarled and half-dead, defying its centuries. Children had played in it for years – she and Stephen had often swung from a rope precariously fastened to one of the lower branches, once indeed she had narrowly missed broken bones when she had slipped and fallen. They had used the hollow trunk – where Royalist Rupert was supposed to have hidden – as a den, had stayed there on summer evenings until creeping shadows had sent them running for home. Now, as she approached it, her collar turned against the rain, she heard young voices . . . real? imaginary? she could not tell . . .

'I can't . . . it's too high . . . I'm frightened . . .'

'Don't be daft. Here . . . take my hand . . . I won't let you fall. There you are. Safe as houses. You can do anything you want if you try . . .'

The clouds were drifting, mistlike, seeming almost low enough to touch. The grass was wet, the ground soggy. 'Mum'll kill me if I get my new socks wet . . .!'

'I'll give you a piggy back. Off we go!'

The sound of other light, childish voices grew louder. Through a veil of rain she saw two small figures, a boy and a girl. The girl was running away from the tree, wet dark hair flying, breathless and squealing with excitement. The boy dashed after her, a thin, ungainly lad beyond childhood but not yet into the substance of young manhood. As he caught up with his companion she shrieked with laughter. He threw an arm about her shoulders and they were gone, disappearing into the drifting rain.

Kate stood stock still.

It's me. I'm going out of my mind.

The thought drifted around her as the rain drifted desolately across the landscape. Behind her, safe and solid, Sheldon Hall was lit with warmth in the sad summer dusk, its windows one by one glowing with lamplight.

I'm going mad.

She was well aware that it was not the first time that the thought had occurred to her in these past, fraught days. It had hovered on the edge of consciousness, unacknowledged, for some time, but now resolutely refused to be ignored.

She had seen in those children the ghosts of herself and Stephen. She had seen, in the rider on the evening that she had met Jaimie, the ghost of Stephen. She forced herself to think on, to analyse.

What else might she have done?

Wasn't it possible that guilt had distorted her view of reality as a fairground mirror might distort the human form? Hadn't she read somewhere that that could happen? Wasn't it possible that she herself had hung that dress – the dress in which Stephen had so loved to see her, that she had been wearing on the evening he had died – in the wardrobe as a punishment, as a goad to conscience and to memory? Had she, even, unconsciously, placed his picture on her bedside table as a reminder – a warning? and if she had done those things – if she had in fact been responsible for all the strange things that had been happening around her – what did it mean? Might she truly be going mad? What was madness? Loving Stephen, dead? Loving Jaimie, living? Loving Jen, and Emily? Loving anyone?

She leaned wearily against the ancient tree, her brown head pressed painfully against the ravaged, living bark. Her hair hung in wet rat's tails about her face. In ten days she had not seen Jaimie alone. She had endured a pleasant evening in his company with Jen and a couple who were old friends of the Lesters, and had shown it, unconsciously cruelly from Kate's point of view, for she felt even more of an outsider listening to the small, shared jokes and remembered anecdotes. Later in the evening, perhaps predictably considering the situation and the way the wine had been flowing, she and Jaimie had argued acrimoniously about – she flinched now to think of it – the role of a woman in modern marriage. The under-current had been there, as always, between them, in this instance sparking something close to animosity. He had said nothing of any personal significance, not even when, alone, he had escorted her to the door. She knew with sure instinct that he felt the next move to be hers. Stubbornly and miserably she would not make it. That night, when she had re-entered her apartment she had switched on the light with a sense of foreboding, searched with almost manic intensity for the sign that Stephen had watched – had read her innermost thoughts. And – inevitably – had found it, though almost she had missed it, so subtle was the rebuke. A small Mason jug had stood square upon its shelf. She had walked to it, just a little unsteadily. She hated it like that. She always had. But Stephen had preferred it straight. They had had, on tired evenings, the occasional silly row about it . . . 'For God's sake, Stephen, that thing looks awful, square like that. It needs to be at an angle! Do leave the damned thing alone!' And now it stood, square to the world. She had regarded it, wine, worry and weariness flowing about equally in her blood, then reached a hand and shifted it just that fraction that it needed to put it right. Now she wondered . . . had she shifted the thing herself? She was beyond knowing, almost beyond caring. She knew neither what she wanted nor what she did not want. For . . . if Stephen were truly haunting her, did it matter? Wasn't that what she had begged for, prayed for, in the months that had followed his death?

Tiredly she pushed herself away from the tree and, head down against the drenching mist, plodded back to the house.

There was a note awaiting her, written in an untidy scrawl that, although she did not know Jaimie's writing, somehow surprised her not at all. She looked at it for a long time, then, composedly, she changed her wet clothes, rubbed her hair with a dry towel and sat down in silence to wait.

He came half an hour later, tapping softly at the door.

'It's open.'

He smiled to see her sitting there, that open, sunny smile that he shared with his daughter. Swiftly he crossed to her and bent to kiss her cheek. 'Mohammed,' he said, lightly, 'has come to the mountain.'

'Where are the others?'

'They've gone to see Jen's mother. The old lady hasn't been too well.'

'But you got out of going?'

He did not seem to notice the strained note in her

voice. 'Yes. As a matter of fact my excuse was perfectly genuine. I really did have work to do.' He kissed her again, touching her hair. 'Your hair's wet.'

'I've been out walking.'

'In this? Idiot. You'll catch your death of cold.' The teasing affection in his voice melted her quicker than any passionate advance might have done. Suddenly, with that quick and unpredictable change of mood that seemed to characterise her lately, she was wonderfully glad he was here. An hour to themselves, he had said in the note. What could possibly be wrong with that? She reached a hand and he pulled her from the chair, slipping an arm about her waist, kissing the top of her damp head. She relaxed against him for a moment. 'Would you like a drink?'

'Mm. Please.'

She stepped away from him, to the table where the drinks stood. 'Gin and tonic?'

'Fine.'

She took the glasses from the shelf, ice clinked, and she reached for the bottle of gin. She had the screw cap half off before she noticed the scrap of folded paper that had lain beneath the bottle. The bottle hit the corner of the table as it dropped from her hand and bounced unbroken to the floor, where it lay oozing liquid out of the loose cap onto the carpet.

Jaimie made a dive for it. 'Kate . . . what on earth . . . ?'

She had stepped back from the table and was staring in undisguised distress at the scrap of paper. Brown around the edges, one side of it rough, as if it had been carelessly torn from a larger sheet, nothing could have looked more normal. He reached for it.

'Don't touch it! Don't!' Her voice was on the perilous edge of hysteria.

'Kate!' He put an arm about her shoulders. She was trembling violently. 'What is all this about?'

'Oh, God.' She buried her face in her hands.

His face a picture of disquieted puzzlement, Jaimie stared at her, looked back at the piece of paper, then very determinedly reached for it. She recoiled from him, several stumbling steps. He opened the note, regarded it thoughtfully, the frown on his face deepening to something close to anger. 'What in hell's name's this supposed to be? Some kind of joke?'

She turned away, dry eyed. 'Read it out.'

He was silent.

'Let me do it for you, then. It says "Love you for ever. S." Am I right?'

'Yes. How do you know? You didn't even pick it up . . .'

'I've read it before. Often. Stephen wrote it on our honeymoon. We were in France, touring in Provence. We stopped for a picnic in a field of wild flowers. Stephen picked me a bunch. Put that note in it.'

'Then what the devil is it doing here?'

She shook her head, one hand pressed hard to her mouth.

'Kate? I don't understand any of this. What is it? What's going on? How did this note get under the bottle? Kate . . . answer me.'

'I think . . . I'm afraid . . . that it's very possible

that I put it there myself.' Her voice was a stranger's, yet oddly composed.

'*What?*'

She moved her head sharply, a distracted, half-angry gesture, almost resentful of the need to explain, even to him. 'I don't know. I don't understand myself what's going on. I don't really believe what's going on. But I'm very afraid that I may be heading for . . . some kind of nervous breakdown.' She lifted her head, her eyes searching his face. 'You do things . . . stupid things . . . without knowing it, if you have a breakdown, don't you?' The words were suddenly pathetic. Tears were rolling unchecked down her cheeks. 'The alternative . . .' she stopped.

'What alternative?'

She hesitated, her hands clasped so tightly before her that the knuckles stood like bare bone. 'Do you believe in ghosts?'

'No.' The word held no doubt whatsoever. Comprehension dawned in the blue eyes. 'Oh, Kate, no. You can't possibly think that Stephen . . .' He strode to her, put an arm about her. She leaned to him, sobbing as if her heart were broken, her overstretched self-control snapping at last like a strained wire.

'I don't know. I . . . *don't* . . . *know!*'

Through her own incoherently sobbed words she heard his voice, disjointed words and phrases, soothing, fiercely tender, '. . . not my sensible Kate? . . . working too hard . . . and the strain of . . . oh, Kate, darling, I'm sorry, this is all my fault . . .'

'No.' She shook her head miserably. 'It isn't.'

His arms tightened around her. 'You must stop this, my darling. You've worried yourself into such a state you're making yourself ill! Everything's going to be all right. You're overwrought . . . torturing yourself . . . oh, Kate, Kate . . . !' She felt the sudden urgency in him, recognised her own need that rose to meet it. Their kiss blotted out everything but that – Jen, Stephen, confusion, unhappiness, were for one blessed moment forgotten in the pure physical pleasure that his touch gave her. She clung to him, willing him to use his strength to wipe out the images of fear in her brain. She did not know which of them moved first towards the door; they were one body, and their need was mutual.

The bedroom lay in the shadowed darkness of late evening. Rain drifted still across the open parkland and wet the windows like tears. They made love fiercely, each drawing the other to a kind of frenzy that defied reason and overrode guilt. They lay afterwards for a long time in silence.

'I should go,' Jaimie said, at last.

'Yes.' She was lying on her stomach, her forehead pillowed on her crossed arms, her face hidden.

'Kate?' Very gently he ran a finger along the curve of her back.

'Yes?'

'Are you all right?'

'Yes.'

He came up on one elbow, trying to see her in the darkness, then reached over and switched on the dim bedside light. 'Are you sure?'

She turned her face to him at last. It was streaked with tears. 'I'm sure.'

'Darling, don't cry.' His quiet voice was distressed.

'Men never understand a woman's tears.' Her slow smile lit her face to brilliance. 'It isn't that I'm unhappy, I promise. Quite the opposite.'

He looked at her for a long time. 'Kate, we have to see each other sometimes. Like this.'

She turned on her back, stared up at the ceiling, her arms lying relaxed above her head, her face strangely serene. 'No. I don't think so.'

'Please.'

'You said it would happen naturally – and it did. I didn't intend to make love with you this evening. Far from it. Another time . . . the deception . . . the necessary lies . . . I'm afraid it would spoil it. Kill it. I couldn't bear that. Nothing's worth it. Not even this.'

In the silence he reached a hand to stroke her breast, and she stirred, turning her head, smiling.

'Kate?'

'Mm?'

'Listen – what you were talking about earlier. These . . . well . . . these odd things that you think are happening . . .' he felt her whole body stiffen. She sat up abruptly and reached for her clothes. 'Wait,' he said, 'Kate, listen to me. Don't you think it's because you've been working too hard? You've been under a terrific strain lately, what with one thing and another. Don't you think that what you need . . .' he paused, watching her, '. . . is a few days away somewhere? Away from here, away from everything . . . somewhere where there's peace and quiet, and lots of sky? Don't you think that might do you some good?'

Her movements slowed. She looked at him, her dark eyes unfathomable. 'What are you saying?' she asked at last.

'I thought . . . supposing I could get away for a few days? A friend of mine has a cottage . . . in the Lake District. No one would know. No one. If I could arrange it . . . just a few days . . . would you come? Would you, Kate?'

She did not answer for a long, long time. He watched her, trying to fathom the thoughts behind the dark, distant eyes. Then, 'Yes,' she said, simply, 'I'd come.'

Later, in the empty flat she sat, drink in hand, in the sitting room in the pool of light thrown by the single lamp that she had switched on. Her face was very calm. The shadowed corners of the room frightened her no longer, and for the first time in days she regarded Stephen's picture with perfectly steady eyes.

Stephen – she spoke within herself, his warm, living image so clear in her mind that the words came as naturally as true speech – please understand. I'm not superhuman. You of all people would know that. A few days, and no more. After that I'll finish it, I promise. Did I ever break a promise to you? Just these few days, and then I'll tell him. He isn't mine. He can't ever be. I know that. But – what harm can it do to take a few days of his life for my own? Jen – and Emily – have him for always. Just a few days together, and then I'll end it. I know it's the best way. For all of us. But, please, Stephen, don't begrudge me this? I wouldn't – if it were you that needed this. A few days and – I promise – I'll come back . . .

Stephen watched her with his faint, unreadable smile.

It all proved easier than she would have believed possible, so simple that it seemed that the gods were on her side at last. She passed the next week in a strange state of detachment, as if some part of her had withdrawn to the safety of the fortress within her head and watched while some other self worked, ate, slept, laughed. She went shopping with Jen to help her choose some new clothes, accompanied the Lesters to a gymkhana in which Emily was riding. Emily, she was pleased to see, seemed after all to have settled in well to the new school that she had so dreaded attending, and sometimes now Kate saw her in the company of girls of her own age, which pleased her immensely. The child needed that – she was perhaps too much in the company of adults. But there were still those moments of companionship between herself and Jaimie's daughter in which she had come to believe in an odd way her own love for Jaimie was rooted. Had she not already loved Emily, would the girl's father have found such a swift way to her heart? She could not know. She discovered too that her feelings for Jen, far from weakening or being tainted by doubt, had strengthened. Her determination that the few days with Jaimie would be all that she would ask held firm;

her relationship with Jenny was something apart, and she fought determinedly to keep it so. Whatever the cost – and surely, the cost would be hers rather than his, for he had Jen and his family – she would give Jaimie up. She promised that to Stephen, and indirectly to Jenny, in her heart whenever the shadow of guilt darkened her mind. She did not try to see Jaimie alone, or to contact him privately. In her odd, fatalistic state of mind she was willing to let the future take its own course until her turn came to guide it. The longer their promised idyll took to come, the longer she had to dream of it. After, it would be finished. She walked in the park, sat by the lake, waiting, hardly thinking, in a state of suspension, neither happy nor unhappy. One evening, as she sat on the fallen tree, softly and hauntingly over the water came the whistled notes of a simple, familiar tune. She lifted her head, listening. The sound was uncertain, caught on the summer evening breeze. It faded, lifted again, died.

She stayed for a long time that night, watching the dark, mysterious glass of the water. When she turned to go back to the house she was singing, softly, under her breath, '*In Scarlet Town, where I was born . . . There was a fair maid dwelling . . .*'

Two days later Jaimie told her that he had got hold of the cottage in the Lakes for a week, starting the following Saturday.

'Is it too short notice? Can you get away?'

'Yes. It's all right. I rarely take any time off. No one will mind.'

'The kids break up on Friday. Jen's taking them to

her mother's for a week – the old lady's been nagging her to go over there for ages. Reckons she's at death's door again. I've said I have to go away on business. It means . . .' he hesitated, looking at Kate a little doubtfully, '. . . it means that I can't actually join you till Monday. Will you mind that?'

'Not at all,' she allowed herself a faint smile, 'I'll go on Sunday. I'm quite used to being alone.'

And would be used to it again.

CHAPTER SEVEN

Kate had never been to the Lake District before, though she had often been tempted, and had guessed from pictures she had seen that she would like it. From the moment she sighted the distant, rain-misted blue peaks she knew she had been right. By the time she found herself driving through the green valleys, with their lakes and woodlands bathed in the strange, diffused, water-bright light that she was to discover was both the most intangible and one of the most beautiful characteristics of the area she was already head over heels in love with the place, despite the discomfort of the overcrowded holiday roads. With no timetable to keep to, and no one to please but herself she crossed Lake Windermere on the quaint, chain-operated car ferry, and did not begrudge the three-quarters of an hour's wait that it entailed to do so. She lunched in a pub in Hawkshead, then pushed on through Ambleside and up into the high country. She stopped in the afternoon at the only shop in the tiny hamlet of Ennerton. The holiday traffic thundered past, shaking the shop windows.

'Screeside? Why yes – just follow the road on towards the pass for about half a mile, and you'll see a little track on the right. Signed, it is, to the three cottages – Screeside, Lanfell and . . . let me see . . . yes, Scar House is the other one. Go carefully, the track's a bit rough.'

She smiled her thanks.

'You've got some fuel for the fire, have you?'

'I'm not sure.'

'You'll need it evenings, my dear. Even at this time of the year, it gets chilly this high up, at night. We've got logs out the back – 75 pence a sack . . . ?'

'Thank you. Yes, I'll take a couple of sacks. And some eggs, bacon, bread . . .' she made up a box of provisions. 'Thank you.'

In the vast, peaceful countryside the cars of the sightseers still crawled, bumper to bumper along the narrow winding road. Kate joined the queue again and crept the half mile to the turn that the shopkeeper had told her about, doing her best not to worry that her precious few days with Jaimie might be spent on something closely resembling the centre reservation of a well-used motorway.

She need not have concerned herself.

The green track signed to Screeside climbed away from the tarmacked strip of winding road and followed a lifting valley into the hills. Within minutes of leaving the overcrowded road she could see no sign of human habitation – no sign, indeed, apart from a couple of walkers on a distant hillside, of human existence. She rolled the car to a gentle halt and stopped the engine, winding down the window. Water rushed far below her, a white, foaming stream that tumbled from the hillside over short, sheer drops to run, musically busy, over the stone valley-bed. The wind soughed over treeless uplands, clouds rested atop the mountains, wreathing and clinging, wisping into patches of brilliant blue sky. She had never seen anything so beautiful, so peaceful. Below her sheep cropped precariously the sheer, grassed slopes, while above her, bare rock rose majestically. She sat there for a long time, allowing the peace and the windswept silence to seep into her city-clogged brain, until the bite of the upland breeze forced her to wind up the window and start the engine again. Half a mile more of stony track brought her to the three cottages. Scar House stood alone, a square, stone-built house, while Screeside and Lanfell huddled together in neighbourly semi-detachment, their tiled roofs overhanging tiny windows, their stone walls looking as solid as the rock that soared above them. It was darkening already on this sunless side of the mountain, and there were already lights in the windows of the other two cottages. She let herself in to Screeside, carted in the groceries she had bought, set about building a small fire. It was not exactly cold, but the mountain air, even in July, had a bite in it. She cooked herself bacon and eggs and ate them looking out of the kitchen window to a great Peak whose top, cleared suddenly and magically of cloud, caught the dying rays of the setting sun. Tomorrow, Jaimie would come. For now she had a little time to herself, away from the world, and she could not bring herself to be anything but happy about it.

She went to bed at nine o'clock, and for the first time in weeks slept like a log.

He came the following afternoon. He arrived while she was out walking, and was waiting, sitting on the tiny bench by the back door, surveying the view, when she got back.

'Jaimie!' She kissed him. 'I'm sorry. I didn't expect you so early. Have you been waiting for long?'

He shook his head, smiling. He looked ridiculously incongruous in his dark business suit and shiny black shoes. He eyed her outfit of shirt, old cords and sensible shoes with approval, kissed her again. An hour later they were out on the mountainside, scrambling up the scree slope with the summer wind singing in their ears, and the magnificent view changing every time they stopped to draw breath and look. Below them, Screeside was a doll's house, fist-sized. They tramped on into the uplands, stopped to rest in the lee of a huge rock.

'Like it?' Jaimie asked.

'Love it.'

'Happy?'

She looked at him, smiled. 'Very.'

That night they made love beneath the low-sweeping eaves and fell asleep in each other's arms in a darkness that was like black velvet. Kate awoke some time in the night wondering where she was, remembering, smiling. She tried to stay awake for as long as she could, storing memories, but happy tiredness and the mountain air defeated her.

The next day they rose late and stayed around the

cottage. Kate giggled when she saw their two cars parked side by side in front of Screeside. 'No one's going to have any doubts about us!' she said, 'I don't think that married people usually arrive in two cars . . .'

Jaimie grinned. 'Do you mind?'

She kissed his nose. 'Not a bit,' she said, and meant it. 'Tomorrow – could we go for a good long walk? I've been looking at the map – there's a place called Dow Crags – do you know it? It looks as if there'd be some lovely views.'

'Yes, I know it. It's one of my favourite places. Bit steep though,' he eyed her in pretended doubt. 'Do you think you can make it, Townie?'

'Try me.'

They took a packed lunch and drove to the foot of the crags. A hard morning's scrambling walk took them across the high, boggy slopes, past Seathwaite Tarn and up the last steep climb to the razor-crest from where, as Kate had guessed, the view was the most stunningly beautiful that she had ever seen. In panorama before them lay mountain, ocean, lake, and – far, far away, the faint shadow of the sprawling city of Lancaster. Jaimie, panting, threw himself thankfully down, dumping his small backpack on the ground and, for the moment ignoring the view, throwing himself backwards, exhausted, on the springy turf.

She laughed. 'What's the matter with you, Townie?'

He reached for her, grabbed her before she could get away, pulling her on top of him, unable for the moment to do anything except hold her captive there, his hands linked behind her back. With a long, pointed finger she thoughtfully traced the features of his face. 'This is as happy a day as I have ever had,' she said, sincerely. 'Thank you.'

He smiled, knowing it the truth. His skin was flushed with exercise and mountain air, his hair blown to a fair tangle by the wind. She sat up. 'Now for the banquet. Chicken sandwiches and Kendal Mint Cake. Couldn't do better at Buckingham Palace . . .'

The walk along the crags was spectacular. On occasion the rocky ground dropped sheer from their feet in frighteningly vertiginous beauty. When they reached the point where the path branched, back and down, towards the road where they had left Jaimie's car, they stopped for a while to rest, perched upon a windy rock, drinking in the almost incredible grandeur around them. As so often happened in this part of the country, the weather was changing rapidly. Over the mountains to the north threatening clouds were gathering, rolling towards them, shadowing the landscape, painting it with a sombre beauty that was no less breath-taking than that which the sunshine lent it. There was a sudden truly chill edge to the wind.

'We'd better get going,' Jaimie said.

'Just one more minute.' Kate sat quite still, holding the moment like a jewel, aware that time, like those dark mountain clouds, was not creeping but suddenly flying by. And, like those clouds, time was bringing inevitable change. For two sweet days they had forgotten the world and its problems. Now, on the horizon, she saw the shadow of tomorrow and could not help but be sad. Another day, perhaps two, and she would see in his face the things they would not speak of. How to live with, and without, each other after this. How to deceive and lie to someone they both loved. No. Her way was best. He must see that. He must. 'Just one more minute,' she said, again.

On Wednesday they walked the length of Ullswater, over the sweeping tops and then, in a Lakeland drizzle that had been threatening all morning, took the lake steamer back to where they had left the car at a village called Pooley Bridge. In the village, Kate went into a small grocery shop to replenish their dwindling supplies. Being served more quickly than she had expected she came out into the drifting rain to find Jaimie gone from the car, where he had been waiting. She dumped the supplies into the boot and looked around. He was nowhere to be seen. She pulled up her cagoule hood, shoved her hands in her pockets and wandered slowly down the road, back towards the lake. He could not have gone far.

He had not. He was in a call box, not far from the shop, talking earnestly into the telephone. Kate stopped short, her heart sinking. There was something – she hesitated on the word – furtive about the way he stood, his head ducked, his back to the road. Beyond any doubt she knew who he was ringing. She could almost hear the conversation '. . . you know what these damned business trips are . . . much rather be with you and the kids . . .'

Before he saw her she turned and rapidly retraced her steps to the car.

She was very quiet on the way back to Screeside. If Jaimie noticed, however, he made no comment. It was not until they had run through the rain from the car to the cottage, unpacked the food that Kate had bought and were settled in front of a newly-lit and more than welcome fire that he asked, 'Is something wrong?'

She had waited all the way home for him to mention the phone call, but he had not. 'No,' she said.

'You're very quiet.'

She did not reply.

'I'm cooking dinner tonight. Steak and chips okay?'

'Fine.'

'Well, that's good, because that's all that I can cook.' He eyed her, waiting for her smile. She obliged, but not over-enthusiastically.

'Tell you what – come and have a glass of wine with me in the kitchen and watch the chef at work? You might learn a thing or two . . .' He was trying harder than she was.

She followed him into the kitchen, accepted with polite thanks her glass of wine. He busied himself with the steaks, salting and peppering them with a flourish, pounding them with more strength than expertise with a heavy wooden rolling pin that he had found in one of the drawers.

'How was Jen?' Kate asked, quietly.

The rolling pin remained raised. He looked at her, carefully lowered it to the table. 'Ah,' he said, sudden understanding in his voice.

'Well? How was she?'

'Fine. Her mother isn't as bad as she cracked on to

be. As usual.' His tone was neutral, his eyes wary.

'I see.'

The silence was difficult.

'Kate, I . . .'

'Yes?'

He shook his head.

'Why didn't you tell me?'

'It didn't seem important.' He knew his mistake the moment the words were out. He coloured.

She looked at him levelly. 'Don't be ridiculous.'

'Look . . . Kate . . . I'm sorry. But you're making too much of this. Of course I rang Jen. I always ring her when I'm away. It would have looked . . . wrong . . . if I hadn't.'

'I realise that.'

'Then what's the matter?'

'Can't you see? *You didn't tell me*. Even here, it's followed us. The deception. The lying and the cheating. Only here we lie to each other . . . by omission if not by commission . . .'

He crashed the rolling pin onto the steak with enough force to drive it through the table.

She turned and left him, walking back into the little firelit living room, sitting in the shadows watching the flickering flames until he joined her with a couple of trays upon which rested plates, knives and forks.

'It's a bit charred, I'm afraid. Lap job okay?' He was falsely bright.

She waited until he had fetched the bottle of wine from the kitchen. 'Jaimie, I have to tell you something. I wasn't going to say anything until later . . .

until tomorrow night . . . but . . .'

'What is it?'

After all the days of thinking, of planning, her careful words deserted her. She sat like stone, staring in misery at the fire, her meal untouched, almost unnoticed on her lap. 'I won't be seeing you again after this week. Not . . . like this.'

He made a sharp, exasperated sound. 'Oh, Kate! We aren't going to go through all this again?'

'No,' she said sharply, 'we're not. I mean what I say. I've meant it from the first. It's the only way. I love you, and I won't spoil it. I love Jen, and I won't hurt her. After this week I want us to be friends . . . yes, friends!' she repeated fiercely at his disbelieving bark of laughter. 'I promised . . .' she hesitated, '. . . myself that I'd do it, and I will. Today's just convinced me that I'm right. It won't work, Jaimie. Not like this. Not now, not ever.'

Very, very carefully he laid his tray aside, came to her, lifted hers from her lap. 'Blame yourself if your dinner gets cold,' he said, and as easily as if she had been a featherweight pulled her down with him onto the rug in front of the fire.

'Now. Tell me again,' he said later, savagely quiet, leaning above her, firelight glinting in his eyes.

Still trembling from their lovemaking she turned her head away. 'I mean it, Jaimie.'

The next day, tramping the mountains in the drizzle he argued and cajoled, lost his temper and all but begged in turn. 'You're crazy, you know that?'

'Perhaps.'

And then she saw the thought take root in him that she did not really mean it – that despite the constant, stubborn repetition of her determination it was simply a female whim, a desire to punish him, for not having told her that he had rung Jenny. She stopped arguing – knowing that inevitably in the end he would have to believe – and their last evening together was more peaceful than it might otherwise have been. She did not think he even noticed her tears as her body opened to his this one last time and love surged between them.

He left the next day, after lunch. Strangely, it was with a sense almost of relief that she watched his car bump down the stony track, back towards the road. There was, she found, already an odd sense of unreality about the whole week now, in which the happiness of those first few days gleamed fitfully like sunshine through the mountain mists. It was hard to believe that the next time she saw him it would be back at Sheldon Hall, with Jen, and Emily, and Ben around him; that, from now onwards, she must school herself to seeing him like that for the rest of her life.

That night, for the first time in a week, she dreamed of Stephen.

The journey home was difficult, the motorways crowded, the weather at first bad, though as she moved south it improved steadily. She always found motorway driving dull, and was glad when she found herself on the Hertfordshire roads, heading for

Sheldon Hall. As if by arrangement the first sight that met her eyes when she turned the car in to the massive iron gates was that of three familiar riders, one on a fat little pony. She stopped the car, for they had already seen her and were heading towards her at their respective paces. Emily raised a delighted hand and urged her horse into a gallop, Jenny and Ben followed more sedately. Emily sat her dancing mount with ease, her face bright with pleasure.

'Kate! We thought you weren't coming home till tomorrow! Where did you decide to go after all? Did you have a nice time? What did you . . .'

'Whoa!' Kate laughed, stopping the breathless flow of questions.

Jenny arrived, smiling widely. 'Hello, Kate. Did you have a nice time?' She was dressed in Kate's riding clothes, her hair smoothed beneath the flattering peaked cap, her brown eyes warm with friendly welcome.

'Lovely, thank you.'

'Where did you go?'

There seemed no reason not to tell the truth. 'The Lake District.'

'Oh, you lucky thing! It's ages since we've been there. I love it. We haven't been back there since Ben was a baby. I'll have to get Jaimie to take us . . .'

'Did you . . .' Emily began again.

Behind Kate, a neighbour's car drew up. He waved cheerfully and waited, unable to pass. 'I'll have to go,' Kate said quickly and in some relief. 'I'll see you later.'

'Can I come?' It was Emily, still riding beside the

slowly moving car. 'I haven't seen you for a proper talk for *ages* . . .'

'Emily, do leave Kate alone . . . she's only just this minute got home . . .'

'Please?' Emily begged.

'Of course. See you back at the house.'

Beaming, Emily cantered off towards the stables. Kate lifted a hand to Jenny and drove down into the sunken drive towards the massive pile of Sheldon Hall. Two men were mending a battered five-bar gate halfway along the lane. One of them lifted a hand to her. She smiled, nodded, memories flooding back. The Devil's Leap – that she had perfected on Rainstorm, that Stephen was always afraid of; over the high hedge, into the lane, two strides then up again, over the gate and away – a dangerous trick at the best of times, she realised now, but impossible with the drive to the house now in constant use. No one would ever jump the Devil's Leap again, that was certain. Perhaps no one ever had before? The thought gave her an absurd sense of satisfaction.

When she entered the flat she stood for a long time in the deathly silent sitting room, listening, searching with her eyes. Nothing was out of place. Slowly she went from room to room. Serenity reigned. Nothing had been moved. It was all right. As she had been certain it would be.

Emily joined her while she was unpacking. 'Shall I make you a cup of tea? Did you have a good time? Did you . . .' she glanced mischievously from beneath sweeping, saffron lashes, '. . . meet anyone?'

'Yes, please, and yes, thank you, and what do you mean . . . "meet anyone"?'

Emily laughed. 'You know . . . anyone nice? Like a man. Like . . .' she cocked her head, eyes bright, '. . . like Robert Redford?'

'No, Emily dear, I did not meet Robert Redford. If I had, do you think I'd be back a day early? What about you? How's your week been?'

Emily had moved into the kitchen, and her voice drifted back over the sound of water from the tap and a clatter of cups. 'Oh, not so bad I s'pose. Bit boring. You know what a drag poor old Grandma can be. Always making out she's at death's door . . .'

Kate opened her mouth to remonstrate, then closed it again. She could hardly blame Emily for repeating what Kate had heard both Jen and Jaimie say often before.

'Dad says she'll outlast the lot of us.' Emily had reappeared at the door. 'And I think he's right. It was a shame, really, that we had to go. I missed the end-of-term disco *and* Sharon Robinson's birthday party.'

Kate straightened, smiling. 'I'm so glad that you've settled down so well. Made friends. I told you you'd be happy, didn't I? And I was right, wasn't I?'

To her surprise, the girl did not answer at once, but turned sideways, leaning against the doorjamb, her hands behind her back, her head tipped back so that her profile was etched against the light. From this angle her face looked strangely shadowed, strangely adult. 'Happy?' she said in an odd tone of voice, and shrugged, 'I s'pose so.'

Kate regarded her questioningly. Emily did not look at her. With a jerky movement she pushed herself away from the doorjamb. 'Golly, doesn't your kettle boil quickly?'

They drank their tea in the sitting room, Kate sitting in the big armchair, Emily perched on the low windowsill. A fitful sun shone over the parkland. In the distance two familiar riders approached.

'It's your birthday on Monday, isn't it?' Emily asked, suddenly and unexpectedly.

Kate looked at her in real astonishment. 'Yes, it is. How did you know that?'

'You told me the date ages ago. I wrote it in my diary. Are you going to do anything special?'

Smiling, Kate shook her head. 'Cakes for the office is about as exciting as I shall get. We oldsters don't mark the day with quite the same enthusiasm that you young ones do.'

To her faintly piqued amusement Emily seemed to accept that with no reservation. The girl leaned her head close to the window. 'Here come Mum and Ben.'

Kate joined her at the window. 'I'm so glad that Jenny gets so much pleasure out of riding now. She needs something like that, to get her out of the house every now and again. She's certainly got over her nerves from the look of her.'

'Mm. She'll never make a really good rider, though,' Emily said, with the condescending confidence of youth, 'She couldn't manage a horse with any spirit. She's done very well, though, considering . . .'

'I'm sure she's glad to have your approval,' Kate said, drily.

The tone was not lost upon Emily. She grinned impishly. The rather odd mood that Kate had sensed in her earlier seemed to have dissipated. 'She looks a bit like you from here, doesn't she?' she said, after a moment, 'Look . . .'

'That isn't so surprising. We're the same height and colouring . . . well, almost . . . and she's wearing my clothes . . .'

'S'pose so. It's funny that you should look so alike and yet be so totally different, isn't it?' Emily's tone was pensive. Then, suddenly she jumped to her feet. 'I'd better go down and help Ben rub that fat little thing down. He never does it properly. 'Bye. See you later.'

''Bye.'

Kate remained at the window and watched as Emily, tall and graceful-moving, ran from the door beneath her to where Jenny and Ben were walking their mounts across the gravelled space in front of the house. Emily put her hand to the bridle of her little brother's pony and led him around the corner towards the stables. Jen glanced up to the window where Kate stood, waved and followed.

Kate watched them go. If she had had any doubts about her break with Jaimie, they would have been dispelled in that moment, she knew.

CHAPTER EIGHT

Kate's light words to Emily about her birthday had been the simple truth. She awoke to a July-bright Monday morning and, recalling the day, lay for a while remembering other birthdays, more celebrated. The year before Stephen had been killed he had, on an impulse of idiotic genius, taken her to Regent's Park Zoo, where they had spent the day like children, with ice cream and sticky buns, exclaiming over bears, camels, tigers, making faces at the monkeys, marvelling at the stately giraffes, squawking back at the gaudy parakeets. The year before that, on an unexpected bonus from his firm, he had taken her to dinner at the Savoy . . .

The alarm clock went off, stridently. She reached a hand to it, then relaxed back onto the pillows. The bed was warm and comfortable. She could afford another five minutes . . .

The thunderous knock on her front door startled her from a world of half-sleep. She sat up, grabbing for her dressing gown. Still a little sleep-dazed, tying her belt as she went, she made her way into the sitting room and opened the door a crack.

'Happy Birthday to you, Happy Birthday to you . . .'

She gaped.

'Happy Birthday, dear Ka - tie, Happy Birthday to you . . .'

Jenny, Emily and Ben beamed at her. They too were all in dressing gowns and each carried a prettily-wrapped parcel.

She stepped back, running a hand through already tousled hair. 'What on earth . . . !'

'Happy Birthday, darling Kate!' Jen kissed her and gave her an impulsive hug. 'Aren't you going to let us in?'

'Well . . . of course . . . goodness . . . I didn't expect this . . . !'

Jenny laughed happily.

'It was a secret,' Ben said, importantly, 'and I didn't tell you.'

'Well, that you didn't.' Unexpectedly, Kate felt the faint burn of something uncomfortably close to emotional tears behind her eyes.

'Jaimie sends love and apologises. He had to leave early this morning. We didn't think you'd care to be woken up at half past five?'

'Hardly.' Kate was still bemused.

'Happy Birthday, Kate.' Emily kissed her lightly and handed her an envelope.

Kate tore it open, her fingers all thumbs. The birthday card was signed by all of them. 'Oh, how pretty!' She stood it on the mantlepiece, by Stephen's picture.

'Now for the important bit,' Emily said. 'You first, Ben.'

Ben, beaming all over his plump little face, held out his slightly grubby parcel. 'I maked it myself.'

The garishly poster-painted caterpillar made, discernably, from dismembered egg boxes had a cock-eyed expression and a grin as wide as its young creator's.

'Oh, Ben! It's lovely!' She hugged him. 'Just what I've always wanted. Does he have a name?'

The question obviously puzzled the child. The shadow of intense thought flitted across his face, then he smiled and the sun shone again. 'Caterpillar,' he said, as if talking to a half-wit baby.

'Oh, of course. How silly of me.' Very carefully Kate laid the vivid thing upon the table.

'Now me,' said Emily and held out a parcel wrapped in pink with a white rosette decorating it. 'And,' she added with a sideways, affectionately scornful look at her young brother, 'I maked it myself, too.'

The scarf matched the wrapping of the parcel – a delicate pink and white. It was cobweb-fine, and in the corner Emily had embroidered a tiny bunch of white daisies. As Kate held it up it floated like gossamer. 'Emily . . . it's perfect . . .' Kate draped the scarf about her neck over her dressing gown, pausing to admire the effect in the mirror. 'Thank you.' She kissed the girl, who ducked her head in embarrassed pleasure.

'And now . . .' with a shy smile Jenny held out a flat, prettily wrapped parcel, '. . . this is from Jaimie and me. I do hope you'll like it.' There was a faint flicker of uncertainty in her eyes. 'To be truthful,

Jaimie wasn't too sure when he saw it. Emily and I had the idea while he was away, you see, so we couldn't ask him what he thought . . .'

'You mean I had the idea,' Emily was watching Kate with her bright, intense eyes. 'And you will like it, Kate darling, I know you will.'

'I'm sure I shall.' Kate tore off the paper and found herself holding a smaller version of the silver frame from which Stephen watched, this very moment, from the mantlepiece. Already in the frame was a picture of Stephen and herself, on horseback, taken outside Sheldon Hall a month or so after they had moved in. 'It's lovely,' she said, after a moment. 'Really lovely.'

'You're sure?' Jenny was still looking at her anxiously. 'You could use it for another picture, of course, if you'd like. But Emily felt that you'd like that one.'

'Undercover stuff!' Emily grinned, proudly. 'I pinched it right from under your nose!'

Kate laughed, and placed the frame on the mantlepiece, opposite the larger one. 'There.'

'It does look nice,' Jenny said in a relieved voice, 'Now . . . drinks tonight, upstairs, at eight . . .'

'But . . . I was going to invite you . . .'

'Too late. You're already invited. See you at eight. Now . . . we'll have to dash or the children will be late for school.'Bye, Kate. Happy Birthday . . . see you tonight . . .'

It turned out, in the event, to be a much more festive day than she had in the least expected. She arrived at work to discover that a whip-round in the typing pool had provided her desk with a pretty bowl of flowers, and later in the morning her managing director with a broad grin produced an unexpected bottle of sherry which most of the office shared amidst an air of celebration at coffee time. Kate was touched. Their good wishes she felt, if necessarily stereotyped, were genuine. Perhaps, she found herself thinking, she had more friends than she knew? At lunch time the whole of the sales department insisted on taking her to lunch. She arrived home that evening very much happier than she had expected to be. Last year, she remembered, her birthday had been one of the grimmest days of the year, beset as it had still been with grieving memories and regrets. Had all this goodwill been there then, and had she simply not been able to see it? She felt still just a little lightheaded from the wine she had drunk at lunch time, and from the unexpectedly happy day. She hummed as she undressed and pulled on her towelling robe, ready to shower. July warmth drifted through the windows she had thrown open, and birdsong mingled with the shouting of children as they raced, playing, across the field.

She looked at the new photograph on the mantlepiece.

That was where this special day had started – with the loving thought of the Lesters. She had had one, snatched, conversation with Jaimie, yesterday, during which she had quietly and calmly reiterated her determination to finish the affair, and had seen in his eyes, beneath his still-expressed disbelief, the beginnings of acceptance; perhaps, even, of relief. She thought of Jenny's smiling, faintly anxious face this morning, and was glad. She smiled a little to herself, remembering Jen's anxiety about her present. How typical of her to get swept away on an impulsive idea of Emily's and then to have second thoughts . . .

She studied the picture. Ever since she had seen it this morning, some small puzzlement had nibbled at the edge of her mind, but would not be pinned down. She shrugged. No doubt it would come to her. She glanced at her watch. One small drink, she thought, to wish myself a happy birthday, then I'll get myself a snack, and shower ready for this evening.

She was half way to the drinks table when a peremptory knock at the door stopped her in her tracks. Half expecting to find one, if not all, of the Lesters, she opened the door.

A strange young man grinned cheekily. 'Mrs Richards?'

'That's me.'

'Flowers for you.' He produced a bouquet with a flourish.

She took them, not looking at them. 'Good Lord. More surprises! Thank you.'

He grinned again. 'Happy whatever-it-is.' He sketched a salute and was gone.

Jaimie! she thought. And then . . . surely not? He wouldn't be so stupid?

She stepped back into the sunlit room and lifted the flowers to inspect them. Stilled as if to death. White lilies with a small, compact bunch of blood red rosebuds at their heart. The scent of them turned her physically sick. These lovely, repellent flowers were almost a replica of those that she had laid on Stephen's coffin.

She dropped them as the image reached her stunned brain, and stepped back, one hand clamped upon her mouth as if to prevent herself from screaming – yet she knew that had the devil himself appeared before her at that moment she could not have uttered a sound. The flowers lay where they had fallen, in a bright pool of sunshine, innocent, mourning white and the scarlet of gore. A card had fluttered from them and lay, face down, on the carpet. Very slowly she picked it up.

'Love you for ever. S.' Even through the trembling of her hands she could read the words. She squeezed her eyes tight shut. She must not – *must not* – lose control. Think! she told herself, savagely. Think!

And – think about what? shrieked another, less stable part of her mind – think about what?

She forced herself, calmly, to look at the card again. The flowers, for the moment, she could not bring herself to touch. Breathing slowly and deeply, fighting the sickness that rose in her throat, she studied it with desperate concentration in an effort to bring herself back to reality. It was a simple piece of pasteboard, decorated and bordered with badly-executed forget-me-nots and rosebuds. The florist's name – a shop she knew in Cravensford – was printed on one side, on the other the scrawled message in an unfamiliar hand – presumably that of the shop assistant. And – she paused – in one corner, a set of figures scribbled faintly in pencil. She held the card to the light. '4/7 for 8/7.' She frowned. '4/7 for 8/7'? And then it came. Today – her birthday – was the eighth. The eighth of the seventh month. Thursday had been the fourth. The fourth of July, for the eighth of July. Thursday had been the day the flowers had been ordered.

Thursday.

On Thursday she – Kate – had been in the Lake District with Jaimie. This, then, was no mad, unconscious doing of her own. It couldn't be. This was deliberate and terrible mischief. And – if this – what else?

The flowers still lay upon the floor where she had dropped them. She walked past them to the chair and sat down, her hands still clasped about the cheap pasteboard card, her eyes upon the sunlit distance. After a long time she stood up and walked to the phone.

'Jen? Jen . . . It's Kate. Look . . . I'm sorry, I'm afraid I can't make it for drinks tonight after all. No . . . I'm not very well. A touch of tummy trouble . . . no, not too bad, but if it's a bug I'd hate to bring it up to you.' Her voice sounded awful. She trusted to the telephone to distort it. 'Yes, it is a pity. Yes, I will. Thanks . . . yes . . . 'Bye.'

She could not stand to see anyone tonight. She walked to the mantlepiece, propped the card up against the silver picture frame where she could see it, then sat down again. She sat like a statue for a long time as darkness gathered about her and the rays of the sinking sun glimmered on the waxen lily blooms as they lay on the floor at her feet.

The clear description that the somewhat surprised shopgirl gave her was unmistakable. Almost she had expected it, but still it turned her stomach and slowed her blood in anguish. She waited another day before she contacted Jaimie. By the time she dialled his number she felt numb, almost uncaring. She phoned him at work – a thing she had never done before – and she could hear the astonishment in his voice when he came to the phone.

'Kate? Is something wrong?'

'Yes. I have to talk to you.'

'But I thought you said . . . ?'

'I know what I said. But this is different. It isn't about us. Well, only indirectly.'

There was a sudden silence. 'Kate,' he said, carefully, 'You haven't . . . I mean you aren't . . . ?' he stopped.

It took a moment, preoccupied as she was, for the apprehension in his voice and the meaning of his half-spoken question to sink in. 'What? Oh, for heaven's sake, no. I'm not pregnant.'

'Ah.' He could not keep the relief from his voice. Unreasonably it irritated her.

'When can I see you?' she asked, a little brusquely.

'Well . . .'

'Look, Jaimie, you can surely see that I wouldn't be asking if it weren't important to me? I must see you. Could I come up to town? Meet you from the office, perhaps . . . ?'

'No. Best not.' She heard the desperate perplexity in his voice at her urgency. 'Look . . . the day after tomorrow Jen's taking the kids out for the day, to do some shopping. She'll almost certainly call in on her mother on the way home. If I could get home early . . . ?'

'Fine. What time?'

'Fivish.'

'Make it quarter past. I can't get away before five.'

'Right. I'll see you then.'

It was a strange, brusque exchange between two people who just a week before had made love before the fire in a cottage half-way up a mountain. Kate replaced the receiver with a sense of loss much greater than she had felt when he had driven away from Screeside leaving her alone.

He was late.

She stood at the window, watching for him, nibbling her thumbnail in a small, nervy gesture. The evening was overcast. She stood like a statue, her eyes on the iron gates, waiting.

Still he did not come.

She turned from the window, paced restlessly from one side of the room to the other, took up her vigil again. Minutes later she turned away once more, wandered through the flat, twitching a cushion here, straightening a curtain there; then back to the window. But still there was no sign of him.

In the back of her mind lurked the memory of another evening like this when she had waited . . . and waited . . .

With a gesture so fierce that the bottle crashed against the glass almost hard enough to chip it she poured herself a glass of wine, took a sip, slammed it down onto the table. It might as well have been vinegar. *Where was he?*

Then, at last, she saw the familiar car swing into the drive and roll smoothly up to the house. Relief, in the space of a breath, turned to anger. It was too bad of him to worry her like this – on top of everything else. By the time she heard his quick, light footsteps on the stairs she was seething, and it was in her face when she opened the door.

He walked into the room warily, as if he were walking on eggs. His face was unsmiling. Whatever he had guessed about the purpose of this meeting he had obviously realised from the tone of her voice on the telephone that it was nothing pleasant. 'I'm sorry I'm late . . . the traffic's terrible . . .' He was in shirtsleeves, his jacket over his arm. He tossed it onto the nearest armchair. His hair was plastered damply to his forehead in the sticky, thundery warmth.

She struggled to control her unreasonable anger. It made no sense to start off on the wrong foot. 'It's okay.'

He was studying her, frowning, his eyes concerned. Having caught sight of her own face in the mirror a few moments before and seen even in her distraction, the shadows beneath her eyes, the straight, unhappy line of her mouth, she was not surprised at that.

'Kate, what is it? What couldn't you talk to me on

the phone about? Why did you want to see me?'

In answer she turned and walked from him into the dining room, motioning him to follow. After a puzzled second he did so. He found her standing in silence before the table upon which the withered flowers lay, still bunched as they had been when they had arrived. The lilies, dying, had filled the room with their sickly scent. The rosebuds had darkened, like old blood, and their leaves were limp and faded from want of water. Jaimie's look of confusion deepened.

'What . . . ?'

She handed him the card. 'Someone sent me a birthday present.' No matter how she tried, no matter how she schooled herself, she could not keep the desperate bitterness from her voice. 'The flowers are almost identical to those I laid on Stephen's coffin three years ago.'

He read it. 'God Almighty,' he said.

'God Almighty,' she said, 'actually had very little to do with it.'

Jaimie's head came up sharply at her tone. 'You mean . . . you know who did?'

'Yes.'

She saw in his face a genuine bewilderment. Suddenly her own bitterness and anger subsided a little, overcome by the knowledge of the pain that she had to inflict on him. 'Jaimie,' she said, very gently, 'it was Emily.'

He stared at her. Shook his head.

'I'm sorry, but I know it was. I went to the shop. The girl's description was absolutely unmistakable.

Tall, slim, fair, pretty. And she said . . .' Kate paused, sucking her lip as if at a sudden stab of pain, '. . . the most lovely smile.'

Still Jaimie said nothing. He looked at the flowers, at the card he still held in his hand. Shook his head again. 'You're wrong. You must be. I don't believe it.' His voice was strangely hard. 'You're . . . you're crazy. Why would Emily . . . Emily of all people . . . do anything as cruel . . . as monstrous . . . as this?'

She looked at him in despair at his refusal to see the obvious. 'Jaimie, can't you see? She must know about us. She must have found out . . . somehow . . . It's the only explanation. This is . . . some sort of punishment . . . I don't know . . .'

He had paled, his skin suddenly bone white. He turned from her and strode to the window, stood with his back to her, the muscles of his shoulders bunched beneath the thin material of his shirt. When he turned his face was haggard.

'I don't believe it,' he said again. *'I won't believe it.'*

'Jaimie! Jaimie . . . you have to believe it. We can't cope with it if you don't. We can't . . .' she checked a little on the word, '. . . help Emily.'

He stared at her as if she had been an offensive stranger. 'Are you sure it's Emily who needs help!'

She tried to ignore that, took a long, calming breath. The reek of the flowers almost choked her. 'Come into the other room. Sit down. We have to talk calmly. And – Jaimie – you have to believe me. You surely don't think I'm making it up?'

The hateful, cold expression was still on his face.

'Didn't you tell me, not so very long ago, that you thought you were heading for a nervous breakdown?'

She might have expected that, but somehow had not. He could not have shocked her more had he hit her. She shook her head, holding down her own rising agitation, knowing too well that if she lost control of herself now all would be lost. 'Come into the other room,' she said again, very calmly.

He preceded her, his swift stride aggressive. She could not find it in her to blame him for his anger. Her own horror at her discovery had been bad enough – how must Jaimie be feeling?

'Please . . . sit down . . . and listen to me. Let me explain what I think has been happening.'

He shook his head, took his stance with his back to the empty fireplace, his feet astride, his arms folded. His fair brows were still drawn together ferociously, yet somewhere within him Kate sensed a desperate uncertainty.

'It isn't just the flowers,' she said, quietly. 'Since I found out that Emily sent them . . . and Jaimie, there is absolutely no doubt in my mind but that she did, the shopgirl's description was Emily to the last curl on her head . . . since I've found out about the flowers I've been thinking. To be truthful, I've been doing very little else. All the other things . . . the moved photograph, the re-arranged ornaments, the dress in the wardrobe . . . Stephen's favourite tune whistled in the park . . . oh, all of it . . . Jaimie, can't you see? Emily's the only person . . . the only person in the world who knows enough about Stephen and me to do it all. She knows almost as much about us as I do! She's seen photographs, heard endless anecdotes, asked endless questions . . . oh, don't you see?'

'I see that you're jumping to conclusions on circumstantial evidence. I see that you're making a theory conveniently fit the facts . . . if facts they are.' He leaned forward, stabbing the air with his forefinger. 'And even if I did take this . . . this nonsense seriously . . . how are you suggesting that she managed it? Are you in the habit of going out and leaving the door unlocked?'

'No, of course not. But Emily had a key . . .'

He pounced on the word. 'Had?'

She nodded. 'She gave it to me back, a few weeks ago . . . when I'd mislaid my own. I lost the spare one last year.'

'Then Emily no longer has a key?'

'No,' reluctantly.

'Then how's the child supposed to have got into this apartment to persecute you? Tell me that.'

Kate got up, walked to where he stood, reached past him to the small silver frame that Jenny had given her for her birthday. She thrust it at him. 'Ask again. Ask how Emily got hold of this photograph? "Pinched it right from under my nose" was what she said. But, Jaimie, she didn't! She "pinched" it while I was in the Lake District with you! The Saturday night before I left I tidied up the last of the photographs that Emily had been sorting for me. This one was still there then. I swear it. I SAW it. I left it on top of the pile. That must have been where she found it. Something puzzled me when Jen first gave me this, and now I know what it was. Jaimie, Emily came into this apartment while I was away and took that photo. I'd stake my life on it. She has a key. She must have. The only reason she did nothing more drastic was that I came home a day early. Jaimie . . . she knows all about me . . . about Stephen. She talks as if she knows him. She's the only one who would know the little things, the little, hurtful things . . .' her voice caught on the words, and she had to struggle for a moment, '. . . that would make me think that Stephen was watching me. Haunting me. That might make me believe that I was going out of my mind.'

He was frowning. 'You're looking for explanations. Don't you see that? Fitting what you want to believe to what you think you know. What about the horseman that you swore you saw, and that you were so certain was Stephen? You imagined that – Kate, I'm sorry, but how can you possibly be sure that you didn't imagine the other things?'

'Did I imagine the flowers? The note under the bottle?'

He did not answer.

'And what makes you so sure that I didn't see a rider – dressed as Stephen dressed, riding as Stephen rode?' Kate turned and left the room quickly, came back carrying Stephen's distinctive riding clothes, held them up in front of him.

'Emily's a tall girl – almost as tall as Stephen was. Couldn't she have borrowed this? It never occurred to me to look . . . to see if they were gone . . .'

He shook his head. 'I know what you're saying,' he said, 'but I simply don't . . . can't . . . believe it. You're trying to convince yourself that, somehow, Emily discovered about you and me and has been . . .' he paused, 'persecuting you. Punishing you for it? Whilst pretending almost to worship you?'

'Yes.'

He shook his head again, with violence. 'No. It simply isn't in her nature. Kate, you don't know her. You can't if you'd believe that of her. She simply couldn't act like that. She's a child . . .'

'No. That's what we all forget. She isn't a child any more. In some ways she's a woman grown. And her feelings for me – whatever they are, or were – would never outweigh her feelings for you. She idolises you, Jaimie. You're the centre of her life. You, and Jen. I've become a threat to the most important thing she has . . .'

They both heard the sound of a familiar car engine. Kate glanced through the window. 'They're back. You'll have to go.'

He stood up, grabbed his jacket.

'Jaimie?' her sharp voice stopped him halfway to the door. 'We can't just leave it like this. You know we can't. What are we going to do?'

He stood against the door like a man trapped. 'Kate, I know that you're convinced of what you're saying and . . . yes . . .' he added as she opened her mouth to protest, 'I accept that you may be right about the flowers . . . though Emily can't be the only girl in Cravensford of that description. But . . . there has to be some simple explanation. Kids nowadays . . . they've got the weirdest sense of humour. Perhaps it was meant as a joke?'

'A joke?' There was bitter disbelief in Kate's voice.

He rushed on. 'And as for the other things, Kate, forgive me, but you don't know, you can't be sure that they aren't part of . . . some kind of illness . . . some kind of mental disturbance . . . you said yourself . . .'

Downstairs the front door opened. Jaimie fled, pulling the door shut behind him. Kate regarded the panelled wood, her eyes passionate. 'What will it take to convince you, Jaimie?' she asked, softly, of the silence. 'What?'

From beyond the door she heard Emily's clear voice. 'Dad! You're home early . . . how lovely!'

CHAPTER NINE

It was a week of summer storms, of warm, muggy nights and almost tropical days; a week, for Kate, of near-desperation. Her situation was impossible; each time she looked at Emily she felt the acid of anger eating at the love she had felt for the girl, transmuting it, bitterly. Worse, as Jaimie's daughter smiled, laughed, hugged her in that impulsive way that had so endeared her to Kate in the first place, the first stirrings of uncertainty began to move, despite herself, in Kate's mind, and she began to lose confidence in her own conviction, in her own stability of mind. Jaimie had inferred that her suspicions – her certainty – came not from proof but from the sickness within her own mind. No matter how she tried she could not entirely dismiss the thought, and Emily's apparently heedless lightheartedness did nothing to help. In a misery of confusion Kate found herself thinking around in circles – contemplated, in the frustration of impotent inactivity, every rash action from confronting the girl herself to running to Jenny with the story. But always the same single fact presented itself and prevented any such action; Jenny must never discover what had been going on, must never know that her daughter had cause for any persecution of Kate.

Jaimie, Kate knew, was avoiding her, and in honesty she could not blame him for that. She became jumpy and short tempered, searched the apartment feverishly each time she entered it for some sign that the girl had been about her mischief again. That nothing actually happened in that week after the flowers arrived did nothing however to ease the strain – the possibility was enough to keep Kate's nerves strung like piano wire. As the weekend approached Kate resolved finally that she must do something, something positive, to resolve the situation, at least to bring it out into the light of day before it truly did start to drive her out of her mind. Jaimie was the key, of that she was convinced – if he could be shown that her suspicions were well-founded then surely he could not refuse to help her? But how to do it? If he had refused to believe – or rather had apparently been unable to believe – what she had told him about the flowers, then what would convince him? She went over and over in her mind the events of the past few months, looking for some kind of pattern. When she found one, however faint and erratic, an idea came. It would be a gamble, and Kate was no born gambler, but it was all she could think of. The alternative was to do nothing. And that was unthinkable.

On Sunday afternoon, unannounced, she turned up at the Lesters' door. She had taken particular care with her appearance – her hair shone, her cream silk blouse and beautifully cut beige trousers suited her slim figure well. She saw Jaimie glance up from his

Sunday paper as she followed Jen into the living room, steeled herself against the sudden, unguarded look in his eyes at the sight of her.

'Look who's come to see us,' Jen said, happily. 'Em, dear . . . clear those papers off that chair so Kate can sit down. And Ben, do pick those things up off the floor before someone breaks their neck . . .'

Kate sat, gracefully, watching Jaimie. She could feel Emily's eyes upon her. When she glanced at the girl, Emily produced her most charming smile. Kate could not bring herself to smile back. 'I'm sorry to bother you,' she said, apparently to the room at large, but with her eyes still pointedly on Jaimie. Apart from a brief greeting he had not spoken.

'Bother us? Oh, don't be silly. You're always welcome, you know you are.' Jen, apparently suddenly aware of the disordered state of the room, flitted about picking up toys and newspapers. 'Would you like a cup of tea?'

'No, thanks. Honestly . . . I don't want to put you out . . . I just actually came . . .' Kate paused, gave a small, embarrassed laugh, '. . . to borrow Jaimie.' She almost saw Jaimie's breath stop at that, sensed the sudden, swift lifting of Emily's head.

Jen laughed, delightedly. 'Any time. How long for? I charge by the week, or by the month . . . and he doesn't come cheaply!'

Kate knew her own colour was high. Jaimie had laid aside his newspaper and was watching her, blankly. Emily had picked up a miniature Rubic cube and was clicking it erratically, apparently absorbed.

'I've got a slight problem that I thought Jaimie might be able to help me with.' She looked at Jaimie. 'You were talking about investment plans the other night, at dinner, remember?'

He nodded.

'I wondered if you'd mind giving me some advice? I don't think I'm getting the best out of mine . . . and I'm not sure what to do about it . . . ?' She knew beyond doubt that he would see straight through the subterfuge. He knew her well enough to know that no one had ever managed Kate's investments but herself, and no one ever would. She lifted her head and looked at him, her gaze direct.

'Good Lord! Our Kate asking for help at last!' said Jenny in mock amazement. 'I never thought the day would come! Well, of course he'll help . . . won't you, Jaimie?'

'I . . . well, I'm no expert . . .'

'I only need some general advice.'

'I . . . of course . . .'

'I wondered . . . could you spare me an hour or so now? I thought perhaps we could go for a stroll in the park? It's very hot indoors . . .'

'Well . . . I suppose . . .' Trapped, Jaimie looked at her, confusion and something close to anger in his blue eyes.

She made her first gambler's move. She stood up, smiling serenely. 'I'm sorry. I obviously have disturbed you. It really doesn't matter. Perhaps some other time . . . ?'

Jenny glanced, quickly and worriedly, at her husband. Jaimie jumped hastily to his feet. 'No . . . no really. Of course I can spare the time. Hold on a minute, I'll just get my shoes.'

'Whoever invented this thing,' Emily remarked in a conversational tone, tossing the cube onto the settee, 'ought to be made to sit down and do it every hour on the hour for the rest of his life, as a punishment. Damned thing.'

'Emily!' remonstrated her mother, mildly.

Emily, unrepentantly, looked at Kate. 'Can I come with you and Dad?' she asked, innocently and unexpectedly, 'I feel like a walk. It's so muggy indoors.'

'Well . . . er . . .' This, Kate had not bargained for.

'Oh, don't be silly, Em. You heard what Kate said. She and Dad are going to be talking business. They don't want you chattering away like a magpie.'

'Oh, but . . .'

'No.' Jen used a tone she rarely employed but which both of her children had learned to recognise as final.

Emily's eyes showed a brief flare of rebellion, then her long, fair lashes veiled it as she looked down at her hands, apparently inspecting her smooth nails. 'Okay.'

'Here we are.' Jaimie came back into the room.

Kate, casually, slipped her arm through his, sensed the surprise in his sudden movement at the gesture. For months they had studiedly avoided physical contact in front of others. 'I won't keep him for too long I promise,' she said, lightly, to Jenny and as she turned away caught sight of Emily who had lifted her head and was staring at her father and Kate, her face utterly expressionless.

Outside the door, Jaimie turned on her. 'What in hell's name's this? Have you gone crazy?'

'Sssh!' Kate caught his hand and pulled him with her swiftly down the stairs, talking rapidly, and very low. 'Jaimie . . . please . . . do this for me. If you feel anything for me . . . if you've meant any of the things that you've said over the past weeks, then just do as I ask now. If it doesn't work . . . if I'm wrong . . . then I promise I'll never mention it again.' She saw the understanding dawn in his face, and the resistance. 'Jaimie, *please!*' She was truly begging, and did not care. He hesitated one moment longer then nodded and allowed himself to be towed down the stairs and to the front door. Kate let them both out, slipped her arm once more through his.

'Walk slowly,' she said, 'as far as the corner of the house. We can slip round by the stables and back up the stairs. Please . . . don't look up at the window. I'm sure Emily's watching us.'

'Kate!' He half-pulled his arm away. She hung on to it and unable, short of actual violence, to break free he subsided. 'I won't have anything to do with this, Kate, whatever it is. If Emily sent you those flowers . . . *if* she did . . . then I'm sorry. I've decided to talk to her about it. Ask her . . .'

'She'll deny it, and you'll believe her.'

'Who should I believe? She's my *daughter*, Kate. I simply don't . . . can't . . . believe she'd do anything so . . . so vicious . . .'

She broke in quickly. 'Jaimie, I know how hard it is. But isn't it better to know? And in fairness to me, won't you just see if this works?' They were fast approaching the corner of the house. 'Please, Jaimie, give me just this one chance . . .' They had turned the corner. Kate let go of Jaimie's arm and, without saying more or looking at him, ran swiftly towards the back of the house. Footsteps behind her showed that her second gamble had paid off. He was following.

She opened the back door, sped into the front hall, stood for a moment, listening, at the foot of the sweeping staircase. The house, in the somnolent, thundery heat, was utterly silent. Kate's heart thumped, blood drummed in her ears. Almost she could hear the light, boyish voice – 'Kate? Where are you? Come on, now . . . don't be stupid . . .' Childhood games, childhood memories, sweet and painful. 'I'm a sorcerer . . . I really am, you know . . . and you're a princess I've captured with my enchantments. Do you mind, Kate? Do you mind being under my spells . . . ?'

'Come on!' Committed now, it was Jaimie who caught her arm as she stood as if suddenly frozen at the foot of the stairs and all but dragged her up them.

With fingers that were all thumbs she let them both into the apartment, shut the door quietly behind her, hearing the click of the Yale lock. Then, in silence, they stood and looked at each other.

'I hope you know how stupid this is? And how dangerous?' Jaimie's voice was grim. 'Jen thinks we're out there . . .' he gestured towards the window. 'What if she finds we're not? Have you thought . . . ?'

Kate put a finger to her lips. 'Please, Jaimie, keep your voice down! Yes, of course I know what it would look like. But . . . it occurred to me that . . . if I could tempt her . . . give her the opportunity . . .'

He looked at her in something close to dislike. Then he turned and with no further word dropped into the armchair by the window and stared moodily out, his fingers steepled before him. With a pang Kate remembered that first day she had seen him, tired, dishevelled, sleeping like the dead in that very chair. She had sat and watched him that day and had loved him ever since. Now it seemed that he could hardly bear to look at her. She sat on the sofa, tense and waiting. The final gamble was now.

Nothing happened.

The sounds of the park drifted through the open window – birdsong, a man's voice, the sound of a horse's hooves on the gravel.

Still nothing.

Kate found her fingers ached from clenching them, and her neck felt as if it might snap from tension.

In the chair by the window Jaimie stirred restlessly. 'How long . . . ?'

'Ssh!' Kate held up her hand imperatively, and unnecessarily. They had both heard it – the quiet clicking of a key in the lock. In a flash Kate was on her feet and had slipped through the door that led to the dining room. Jaimie drew back behind the protective wings of the big armchair.

Emily came into the room utterly soundlessly, shut

the door behind her, turned.

Kate was watching Jaimie. She saw for a moment the dawning pain in his face as he admitted to himself the significance of his daughter's presence here. Then, as he stood up and confronted Emily all expression drained from his face. Emily, turning from the door, the key in her hand, froze at the sight of her father, her face undisguisably shocked. Then, with admirable self-control she pulled herself together.

'Why, Dad,' she said, brightly, only the slightest quaver in her voice, 'you scared the life out of me. What are you doing here? I thought you were going for a walk?'

'That's what I wanted you to think.'

Emily spun to the sound of Kate's voice from the open dining room door. Her thin, fair, sunflushed skin was suddenly burning, her eyes very bright. For a long moment, no one spoke.

'I . . . came down to borrow that book you promised me,' Emily said at last, still trying; but her voice was less than certain.

'Why didn't you ask me for it just now, when I was upstairs?'

'I . . . forgot.'

Kate advanced, unsmiling, into the room. 'Emily . . . where did you get that key?'

The girl glanced down at the key she still carried as if she had forgotten that she was holding it. 'This? Why . . . you gave it to me. Don't you remember?'

Kate nodded. 'Of course I remember. But I also remember that the key I gave to you, you gave me back, when I mislaid my own. I have it here . . . in my pocket . . .' She held out a steady hand. Reluctantly Emily dropped the key she held into it. Kate held it up, put her hand into her pocket and drew out the other key, holding the two side by side. Her own key was dull with age and with use. The one Emily had handed to her was bright and new-looking, the edges sharp.

Emily looked at the two keys in silence, her mouth set in a childishly sullen line. 'You took the key away,' she said, 'I felt as if you'd locked me out.'

'Would you have blamed me if I had?' Kate asked, softly, searching her face.

Emily acted as if she had not heard her. 'So . . . well, yes, I did have that key made . . . so that when the winter comes again I can get in to light the fire, and things. You used to like me to do that. I was going to surprise you . . .' Her voice was oddly desolate. Something moved in Kate's heart.

'Why didn't you ask me if you could have a key? Why steal it and copy it?'

'I told you. I wanted to surprise you.'

'You did that all right. Several times,' Kate said, grimly.

Emily did not reply.

Her father took a step towards her. She glanced at him, half-frightened, her blue eyes wide. Jaimie stopped abruptly at the look on her face. Astonishingly, Kate felt anger drain from her as with sudden and unexpected clarity she saw the situation from the child's point of view and could have wept for her. She had been so concerned with her own troubles, so self-centredly determined to convince Jaimie of his daughter's guilt, and to protect Jen from that of her husband and her best friend that she had not looked beyond Emily's apparent spite to the depth of hurt in which it must be rooted.

'Sit down, Emily,' she said, gently. 'We have to talk. Don't we?'

Emily, in silence, perched upon the edge of the sofa, her back very straight, her eyes fixed upon her clasped hands. Since Jaimie's voice seemed to have deserted him entirely, Kate asked quietly, 'Do you want to explain?'

The girl tossed her fair hair from her eyes and lifted her chin, a little defiantly. 'Explain what?'

'Don't play games, Emily. Not now.' Kate glanced around the sitting room. 'What were you going to do this time? Move the photograph again? Shift the furniture? Or had you something new in mind?'

There was a long, long silence. Emily sustained her defiant stance for as long as she could, then, very suddenly she bowed her head, but not before Kate had seen the sudden blurring of those blue, clear eyes with tears.

'Oh, Emily . . .' she said, into the silence, all the tenderness that she had ever felt for the girl in her voice.

The tone broke Emily's defiance as harshness had not. 'It's your fault. The two of you. I saw you . . . I wanted to stop you . . . we wanted to stop you . . . both of you . . . from . . .' Her slim shoulders were shaking, the incoherent words those of a lost child.

Kate glanced in desperation at Jaimie, unable to bear the sight of that lone, comfortless figure shaken with sobs. But Jaimie sat like a statue, staring at the weeping child, his face a battlefield for conflicting emotions, so it was Kate herself who moved to Emily and put an arm about her shoulders. To her surprise – she had more than half-expected the child to pull away from her, or worse – Emily leaned to her for a moment, sobbing heartbrokenly onto her shoulder until, with an obvious effort, she pulled away and sat up, brushing the back of her hand across her eyes. She took a moment longer to control herself, then she turned to look directly into Kate's eyes, her own miserably reproachful. 'You're making it look as if it's me who's done wrong, when you know it isn't. You . . .' she looked from Kate to her father and back again '. . . you were doing something awful, and we had to try to stop you. We . . .' she pulled herself up 'I thought if I tried to make it look as if it were Stephen, then you'd take some notice. I . . .' she hesitated, an odd, baffled expression on her young face as she searched for words 'I . . . sort of helped Stephen. Did the things he would have done, if he could. *He* doesn't want you two to be . . . lovers . . .' her voice cracked in distaste at the word. Kate winced. 'It's horrible. He wants us all to be friends again, wants things like they were before. I *know* he does . . .'

Whatever defence Kate had expected it had not been this. She stared, for the moment nonplussed.

'Emily . . .' It was the first word Jaimie had

spoken, and it was harsh with pain.

Emily turned her face to her father and smiled a tearful, fearful shadow of that smile that Kate so loved. 'I'm sorry, Dad,' she said, softly, and in that moment the last vestiges of Kate's bitter anger left her.

She took the girl's hand in both of hers. 'Emily, please listen. You're right. We know that what we did was wrong. And we're sorry, darling . . . truly sorry that we've hurt you so. It was the last thing either of us would have wanted. But I'd like to try to explain . . . not excuse, but explain . . . and I want you to try to understand. For all our sakes.'

The girl looked at her, waiting, oddly trusting.

'You're right, of course. Your father and I have been seeing one another . . .'

'I know. I was walking in the park one evening. I saw you over by the lake, in a little clearing. I didn't like to disturb you . . . you looked as if you were asleep. Then . . .' she swallowed, 'Dad came. And he . . . kissed you . . .'

'Emily . . .'

The girl rushed on. 'And then, the Sunday after Ben's picnic I saw you again. I followed you, that time. I *knew* you were meeting Dad. I crept round the other side of the lake to the clearing again . . . and he was waiting for you. I *saw* you . . .' she caught her breath unhappily.

Those two meetings in the wood by the lake, that might have been a century since – Kate's grip on the girl's hand tightened, as if by sheer strength of will she would instil understanding. She was aware that something in what the girl had just said had disturbed her, had rung a small, questioning bell in her mind, but for the moment she ignored it. Just now, Emily's understanding was the only important thing.

'Listen to me, Emily. I'm going to try to explain something that you might find difficult to understand.' She paused, took breath, 'Sometimes things happen to you that you don't want to happen. That you don't ask for, or look for. Accidents. Illnesses.' She half-smiled, crookedly, 'Love. I know it must be hard for you to understand, but please believe me, what happened between your father and me was just that – an accident. We were unprepared, and we didn't fight it hard enough. Perhaps, when you're more grown up, you'll forgive us for that. But above all, you must believe that we didn't want to hurt anyone.' She stopped on that, wondering how many times those same words had been spoken in much the same circumstances. Emily watched her earnestly. Kate ploughed grimly on. 'What happened, happened, and yes, we're guilty because we didn't ignore it, didn't turn away from it. But, Emily, you must believe that our feelings for each other never affected our feelings for you, or for your mother . . .' she saw the girl flinch from that, and felt that she had touched the heart of the matter. 'Especially your mother,' she repeated, firmly, and found that she was hating herself as she never had before in her whole life. 'And it's just for that reason that Jaimie and I have already decided that what's between us must stop.'

Emily looked up, quickly and questioningly at that, glanced at her father.

He nodded sombrely. 'That's right.'

Kate was intent upon her task, could not tell from the girl's unfathomable blue eyes if she were winning or losing. 'You're a party to our secret,' she said, 'and I know that isn't fair. I know how much it must have hurt you. Confused you. But can you try to understand that grown-ups get confused too, sometimes? And that's what's happened over the past few months. Emily, it's over. Do you believe that?'

Emily looked at her, uncertainty written on her face. 'You and Dad did go away together, didn't you? Last week? It wasn't a business trip, was it?'

Jaimie buried his head in his hands. Kate bit her lip. 'Yes. We did. But it will never happen again, I promise you. On my life, I promise.'

Emily looked at her steadily, considering. 'Swear on something else,' she said, suddenly.

Kate looked a question.

Emily stood up and ran to the mantlepiece, taking Stephen's picture from it and clutching it to her breast as if it had been her only treasure. 'Swear on this,' she said.

'Emily!'

Kate stopped Jaimie's protest with a swift glance and as steadily as she could manage held out her hand for the picture. Emily extended it. Kate laid her hand on the cold glass. 'I swear,' she said.

Emily lifted the photograph again and looked at it, her eyes soft. 'There . . .' she said, quietly, and, oddly disturbed, Kate realised that it was neither to her nor to Jaimie that the child was speaking.

'Emily . . .' she began uncertainly.

Emily did not look up. Her eyes were still on the photograph, and if that single, softly spoken word had jolted Kate, the expression on the girl's face disquieted her even more now. How had it happened that she had not seen this before? the look in the young eyes was sheer hero-worship. Poor Emily – doubly betrayed – she remembered what the child had said earlier about helping Stephen, remembered the 'we' she had used so often.

'Emily,' she found herself saying softly, the words almost choking her, 'Stephen's dead.'

Emily lifted bright, tear-reddened, surprised eyes. 'Well, I know that. Of course I do. But he's here, too, isn't he? All around. Don't tell me you don't know it. You know you do. You showed him to me . . .'

'I think this has gone on quite long enough.' Jaimie strode to the centre of the room, glowering at both of them. 'Emily, we must get this straight. Do I understand that you're admitting that it is you that has been responsible for the . . . incidents . . . that have so disturbed Kate over the past few weeks?'

'Yes.'

'And did you send her those . . . those diabolical flowers on her birthday?'

There was a momentary pause. Emily sniffed. 'Yes,' she said, very low. She turned to Kate. 'Is that how you found out?'

Kate nodded. 'The florist remembered you.'

'I'm sorry I did it now . . . oh, not because I was found out, but because . . . because I know how horrible it must have been for you . . . but, oh Kate, I was so *angry* . . .' she clenched her hands at the memory, 'when I realised that you and Dad were . . .' she could not go on for a moment. She swallowed, noisily. 'And then . . . when Dad rang home and I thought you might be there . . . in the phone box with him . . . laughing . . .' Tears were very close again. 'I *wanted* to hurt you. I wanted to! But now . . . I'm sorry . . .'

Kate glanced at Jaimie. He stood like rock, his face bone-white. 'I wasn't laughing,' Kate said, quietly, 'I wasn't anywhere near the phone box. I didn't know he'd made the call.'

'What a bloody mess,' Jaimie said, his eyes anguished upon his daughter, 'what a stinking, bloody mess.'

Emily carefully stood Stephen's picture on the table and went to her father, laying her still tear-wet cheek against his. 'I think it's going to be all right now,' she said. 'We've made it all right. Don't worry.'

Kate, disturbed again by that 'we', stood up. 'Jaimie . . . why don't you go upstairs to Jen? Leave Emily here with me for a while . . . if she doesn't mind, that is?' She looked at the girl, who shook her head quickly. 'Say we met her in the park, or something, and I brought her back for tea. Jenny will know there's something wrong if she takes those red eyes upstairs. Give her a chance to recover,' she smiled, a little sadly, at Emily. 'Give us both a chance to recover,' she added.

'Well . . . I don't know . . .'

'Please, Jaimie. We'll be all right now. We need to talk. We've both hurt each other. We can't just leave it at that.' She saw the girl's quick, grateful glance at that, and her heart lifted a little. 'Go on, Jaimie. Tell Jen that Emily will be up later. Please?'

In the silence that followed the closing of the door behind him they looked at each other, suddenly constrained.

'I'm sorry, Emily,' Kate said, and marvelled that just a few hours before she would never have believed she could have brought herself to say those words.

'Oh, Kate! Darling Kate!' The dam burst. Emily threw herself upon Kate, sobbing uncontrollably. 'I'm sorry, too . . . the horrible things I did . . .'

Kate stroked her hair gently. 'Don't think about it any more, my love. Let's just try to forget the whole rotten business. Please believe me . . . it's over. All of it. Try to pretend that it never happened.' And, listening to the convulsive, subsiding sobs she reflected with some envy that Emily was probably young enough to do just that. In the turn of a year the memory would be fading; in two she would be too busy about her own romantic affairs to think of others. And what of me? Kate wondered, bleakly, where am I? Emily will forget, Jaimie has Jen. And I . . . ? She attempted a bright smile into the young, woebegone face that rested on her shoulder. 'You trying to drown me?' she asked. 'Come on, now. Chin up. Worse things happen at sea, you know. Whistle a happy tune and all that . . .'

Emily, wrung out by emotion, tried to laugh and succeeded only in hiccoughing violently, almost choking herself. When the spasm had died she grinned lopsidedly, a gallant attempt to match Kate's determined lightness. 'You know I can't whistle,' she said.

* * * * * * * *

A couple of hours later Kate shut the door behind an almost entirely recovered and back-to-normal Emily and came back into the sitting room, her face pensive. She sat on the sofa, her legs lifted to the small coffee table, her head thrown back tiredly. The storm which had threatened all afternoon flickered luridly on the horizon. Great purple clouds oppressed the sky, muttering dire warnings. A few enormous drops of rain spattered down and in the distance thunder rumbled.

Kate picked up Stephen's picture and looked at it for a long time.

I'm going to have to leave.

Stephen watched her. The unanswered questions fretted faintly at the far edges of Kate's mind. The thunder rumbled nearer. Lightning flickered, lighting the dark room, sending swift shadows racing over the ceiling.

You can see that, can't you? I'm going to have to leave.

Leave Sheldon Hall? Leave Jen – Emily – Jaimie – Ben?

Yes.

The rain sheeted with tropical suddenness. She got up and ran to the window, slammed it down. The sill was already awash. In the vivid, blue-white light of the lightning she walked back to the sofa, sat down again, looking at the photograph.

Leave me?

Yes. Leave everything. Start again.

And no! cried another part of her – you can't!

I must, she answered, intense and calm, I must. The job I was offered in London a little while back – I'll get in touch with them again, see if the offer's still open. The sky's the limit nowadays for a woman who's ready to work hard. I must.

The storm appeared to have centred itself over the park. The turbulent air tossed the trees, thunder and lightning sounded simultaneously. Very gently Kate reached to the photograph and laid it flat, face down on the table. Then she leaned back, her eyes shut, and listened to the storm, trying, unsuccessfully, not to think.

CHAPTER TEN

Kate mentioned to no one her intention of leaving Sheldon Hall. But with dogged determination and half against her own will she set about making plans. She would not move to London without first securing her future. To be homeless would be bad enough – and she could not rid herself of the feeling that, no matter where she lived, away from Sheldon Hall she would be homeless – to be jobless as well would be plainly stupid. But jobs, in this age of unemployment, no longer grew on trees, and the people who had, just a few months before, firmly offered her a position in an expanding business, now with regret told her that the situation had changed and while, hopefully, the opening still remained, the decision to fill it could not be taken for another month or so. And so she had to muster what patience she could and live from day to day, waiting. It was neither a pleasant nor a happy time for her. She was torn between longing to go and needing to stay. Her nights were intolerably restless, her days taut with an uneasy tension that shortened her temper – with herself and with others – and frayed her nerves. It was this, she knew, that imbued her life with the strange feeling of persecution that still haunted her; for, although with Emily once more her friend the disturbing physical manifestations had stopped, she could not rid herself of the ridiculous conviction that in some ways the house and its memories had itself turned against her. She knew, of course, that the feeling was absurd – but in the darkness of night, sound and movement sometimes startled her awake, her heart thumping violently; sometimes she would imagine that she heard a footfall in the hall, or young voices echoing in the stairwell beyond the great double doors, when she knew there were none. Rationally, she understood what must be happening – her guilt about Jaimie, reinforced by what she felt to be her betrayal of Stephen in deciding to leave the house had bred fancies in her own overwrought brain that in times of stress worked on her imagination and wore down her nerves. Yet another good reason to leave the Hall. But she could not deny that this rationalisation sometimes let her down in the long, sleepless watches of night when she found herself thinking of a rider in the park – and of that small, hiccoughing phrase – 'You know I can't whistle . . .'

That she dreamed of Stephen constantly could be little surprise in the circumstances. Many times she woke, her face wet with tears, knowing him gone once more when she had felt, in sleep, that he had been with her. She had suffered something similar to this before, when first he had died; she recognised it now for what it was – yet another symptom of stress. Sometimes she wondered – if she gave up her determination to leave, gave in, so to speak, to the relentless pressure that her subconscious was quite evidently exerting upon her to stay, would these disquieting and – she had to admit it – nervewracking experiences cease? But with stubborn determination she clung to what her good sense told her; peace, now, was somewhere else. She had to leave.

Her decision, however, was a little shaken on an evening half-way through September when a wan-looking Jenny called to see her.

Kate looked at her in consternation. 'Is something wrong?'

Jen threw herself disconsolately into a chair. 'It's Jaimie. It looks as if he's going to have to go away again.'

'Oh dear.' Kate could not for the life of her tell if the sudden churning of her stomach were dismay or relief. 'When? How long for?'

'Quite soon from the sound of it. And for six months at least. Perhaps longer. Oh, Kate . . . I know he has to go . . . it's a good job, and they aren't easy to come by, now, with the industry contracting all the time, but . . .' she made a helpless, miserable gesture with her hands '. . . we've got so used to having him home. And I do so hate it when he's away.'

'Yes.'

'And the children miss him so . . .'

Kate watched her, sympathy in her eyes. Jenny laughed, gently self-derisive. 'Hark at me. I'm acting like a child. He does it for us . . . and with what the flat cost, heaven knows we need the money. It won't be for ever. And . . .' she smiled, warmly, '. . . it isn't as bad as it's been in the past. I do have you this time.'

Kate stood up abruptly. 'Do you have time for a drink?'

'Mm. Please. A G. and T. would be just what the doctor ordered.'

Kate poured the drinks, stood holding them, looking at Jen with worried eyes. 'Jen?'

The other woman lifted her head. 'Yes?'

'Jenny . . . supposing I told you that I was thinking of leaving Sheldon Hall?'

'What? Oh, Kate, no! Surely not?'

Kate handed her the drink. 'I'm tinkering with the idea. There's some possibility of another job. A very good one . . . I don't know for sure yet, but if it comes off I'll be working in London.'

'But . . . you could commute, couldn't you? Like Jaimie does? Kate . . . thousands of people commute from Cravensford, don't they?' Jenny's expression was stricken.

Kate shook her head. 'Honestly, Jen, I just don't fancy that. All that travelling. It's different for Jaimie . . . for most men. They've a home and family waiting for them. Dinner cooked, the housework done. No . . . if I get the job then it really does make sense to move to London.'

'Will you like that?' Jenny was making a valiant effort to swallow her own disappointed distress.

'I don't know.' Kate shrugged. 'I lived in town for a couple of years when I first went out to work . . . while Stephen was away at university. I quite liked it then.'

'But, Kate . . . you *love* the Hall. You know you do. How can you bear to think of leaving?'

A question she asked herself at least a dozen times a day. Kate sipped her drink. 'Things change. Whether we like it or not. I honestly feel that I have to leave.'

'Well . . . if you feel like that then I guess I don't have the right to try to persuade you to stay. But do promise me not to do anything too hastily? Think about it – really think about it – before you make up your mind. I'm sure you'll be miserable away from the Hall.' Jenny reached a hand to her, 'And, oh, Kate, we'll miss you so if you go.'

The weeks stumbled on. Autumn gilded the countryside and the drying leaves rustled in the woodlands like whispering voices. On the day that she learned that the London job was hers, Kate drove home through a golden October evening no nearer to knowing what her final decision was to be than she had been for weeks.

She let herself into the quiet flat. She must decide. Now. She poured herself a drink, leaned by the window, sipping it, looking out across the park.

Could she give this up?

Of course she could: London – theatres, shops, people – would be fun. She'd buried herself down here for too long. With the money she could get for this apartment she would be able to buy a really nice little flat somewhere. Chelsea, perhaps. Or Kensington.

And – no! said that other voice, no!

Impatience moved in her at her own irresolution.

Make up your mind, for God's sake – stay or go. But stop dithering!

Her drink was gone. She poured another, a little stronger, came back to the window. A group of riders clattered below her, from the stables, and headed out into the park at a canter. She had a sudden unexpected urge to be out there with them, in the golden evening sunshine, ridding herself of the pent up physical energy that tightened the muscles of her neck and kept her from real rest. She needed exercise, damn it. Fresh air. The chance to blow the worries away with the cobwebs, to put things into perspective. She was too much indoors, too much alone. She remembered with a lift of pleasure the feeling of freedom that riding had always given her, the refreshing and invigorating excitement of a canter across the park . . .

She tossed the remainder of her drink back in one swallow. Why not? Wasn't her inability to ride just another manifestation of her enslavement to this place and its damned memories? Why not try – now? If she beat that, might she not find that she could beat everything else? Might she not find it easier to come to a decision and – even more important – to stick to it?

She was already at her wardrobe, yanking out a shirt and a pair of old cords. She didn't need to bother with all the gear – she had her boots still, for they had proved too large for Jenny, and there were always spare hats at the stables – Feverishly she pulled off her dark suit and silk shirt, threw them haphazardly on the bed. An odd excitement was growing in her, a confidence born partly, she realised, from the gin but partly too from something deeper. This time she would do it. She was sure of it. She stamped her feet into the boots, tucked her shirt in at the waist, ran her fingers through her hair. Her reflection in the mirror looked ten years younger. The sunshine beckoned. Happy to be active, she picked up the crop that had been Stephen's and left the apartment, running lightly down the stairs and out into the warm evening.

The stables, disappointingly, were almost deserted.

'Hello? Anyone there?'

A horse moved somewhere in a stall. Dust danced, swirling, in a beam of light. The air smelled, thickly sweet, of hay and manure and horse. 'Hello?' Kate walked farther into the gloom of the great block. It had been built perhaps a hundred years before, and had changed little in that time. The stalls were divided by massive carved wooden partitions, atop of which wrought iron reached to the lofty roof. The floor was cobbled, and channelled for water and waste. 'Anyone there?'

A horse's hooves clicked again, restlessly, on the cobbles, and Kate moved to the only occupied stall. 'Hello, old girl . . . fancy a run do you?' This was the mare that Emily sometimes rode, a handsome animal, spirited and strong. Kate put a hand to the powerful neck, feeling the warmth and smoothness of it, suddenly wildly impatient to be away, to be part of this animal, moving as one flying entity. Of the awful, sick nostalgia that had kept her from the stables for so long there was not the slightest sign. Why, oh why had she left it so long?

'Hi. Can I help you?'

Kate turned. 'Ah, yes. I'd like to hire the mare for an hour or so, please.'

The girl who had entered – small, dark, not much older than Emily – looked doubtful. 'I'm sorry . . . the owner of the stables isn't here just at the moment. She's very particular who rides Star. She isn't the easiest mount to manage.'

'Do you have another available?'

The girl shook her head. 'Sorry. They're all out.'

Kate had not come this far to be easily put off now. 'Look . . . I'm an experienced rider. I'm sure I can handle her. I'll take the responsibility with Miss Jenkins, I promise.'

The girl's face cleared a little. 'You know Miss Jenkins?'

Kate stretched a point. 'Very well. I'm sure she won't object to my taking Star.'

'We-ell . . .' The girl's practised eye took in Kate's sensible outfit, the well-worn boots, the slightly decrepit riding crop, 'I suppose it'll be all right. If you know Miss Jenkins. But you'll need a hat.'

'Can you find me one while I saddle up?' Kate smiled her most persuasive smile.

'Sure.' With a sudden grin the girl turned away, waving a hand to the other end of the stable block. 'You'll find all you need over there.'

Ten minutes later, Kate was up on the skittish Star and walking her out into the sunshine. She grimaced a little as she felt already the strain on muscles long unused. She'd suffer for this tomorrow. But she was in the saddle, and that was what mattered. In some way it symbolised a breakthrough, a return to the old, confident Kate. She clucked gently to the dancing mare, and the stable girl watched approvingly and with evident relief as Kate brought the animal under control. She walked the mare out of the stable yard and across the front of the house, feeling the old rapport between herself and the animal she rode, recognising the rise of a familiar excitement at the sense of movement, and strength, and freedom. Everything else had fled her mind – her worries, her unhappiness, her indecision, all were pushed to one side in the pure pleasure of sunshine, lovely surroundings and the relaxation of physical activity.

'Right, old girl,' she leaned to pat the mare's arched neck. 'Easy does it at first, eh? Don't let's try to run before we've remembered how to walk . . .'

She rode slowly across the park, in the general direction of the lake. Children played under the trees. A flight of wild duck had settled upon the water in a sheen of ripples that spread, dancing in the light, to the wide banks. Star lifted her head and paced beautifully, happy to be out. Kate's confidence grew. It seemed hard to believe that it had been three years since she had ridden. She reined the mare in, turned her, urged her to a gentle canter. The swifter movement cooled cheeks that were flushed from the October sun that was dipping now, unexpectedly quickly, to the west. Kate rode on, beyond the lake, to the far boundary of the parkland. Star dropped back to a walk. Kate patted her neck again. 'Good girl.' The mare picked a delicate way down a steep incline towards the stream which fed the lake. By the stream Kate dismounted for a moment, easing already aching muscles. She stood a long time, one arm thrown across the animal's neck in silent companionship, watching the sinking sun and feeling happier than she had in a very long time. She thought of nothing – simply let the beauty and peace of the moment envelop and soothe her. Then she stroked Star's smooth nose. 'I guess we'd better be getting back.'

The sun was almost gone. A few clouds had built in the sky, tinged with the flame of an Indian Summer evening. A drift of woodsmoke smudged the sky and filled the air with its fragrance. Kate swung, a little stiffly, back up into the saddle and set the animal back up the bank towards the lake. As they breasted the rise she pulled her mount to a momentary halt, surveying the mass of the house in the distance, its upper windows still reflecting the red sheen of the setting sun, the waters of the lake dark now, glinting between the autumn-painted trees.

How many times had she and Stephen sat here, when the old house had been theirs – an empty shell – and dressed it in its former grandeur? From this distance glassless windows and missing tiles, cracked brickwork and broken hinges had not been evident, and they had been able easily to see what the place had once been.

Stephen's voice: 'Here come the carriages, see them? There's a pretty one – and look – look at the black one with the pair of matching greys and the splendid coachman. Whose is that, do you think? I'll tell you – it's Lord D'Arcy, come for an evening's gambling and any other entertainment that takes his fancy. The girls had better be on their guard tonight . . . !'

Stephen. As she heard his voice, so she saw him. He rode beside her, laughing. For a moment, had she let herself, she might truly have believed it. Star danced, restlessly. Race you to the house! She found herself, suddenly, urging Star to a canter, to a gallop. The ground flew beneath the little mare's hooves. Too fast. She was riding too fast. The woodland by the lake flashed past. She caught sight of faces, turned to her. Automatically she guided the mare, pushing her on. Faster. Mingled with the thunder of her own mount's hooves she might swear that she heard those of another, overhauling her. Oh, no you don't – she heard her own laughter. She'd beat him to the house – hide from him – She kneed the mare to the left, thundered across the short grass; saw, ahead, the hedge that she knew edged the sunken drive. The Devil's Leap. She could beat him at that, she could always beat him at that . . .

Reality flooded her brain like the rise of icy water. What in God's name was she doing? She hauled on the reins, but the mare was flat out now and would not be stopped. The hedge that hid the drive was almost upon them. Kate, realising there was no way to stop the animal now, yanked the mare's head savagely sideways, trying to steer her away from the danger. Too hard. The animal, unbalanced, reared. Kate clung on for dear life. Star, the bit well and truly between her teeth, bolted, and seconds later Kate was on the ground, every vestige of breath gone from her body and every bone jarred to breaking point. Someone shouted. She heard the sound of running feet.

'You all right, love?'

She sat up. A man's worried face peered down at her, and a dog sniffed interestedly at her boots.

'Yes, I think so.' Her voice shook.

The man's wife joined them. 'Nasty things, horses,' she said. 'Won't get near them myself.'

'No . . . it was my own fault . . .' Kate struggled to stand up, but for the moment her shaking legs would not support her.

'I'd stay down for a bit if I were you,' said the man, sympathetically. 'You went one hell of a thump. You sure nothing's broken?'

'I . . . don't think so.' Gingerly Kate tested her arms and legs. 'No. I'm all right, thank you.' Her trembling was subsiding. In the distance a boy had collected Star and was leading her back. Kate made a more successful attempt to rise and stood flexing sore muscles.

'You lost something, Missis?' the youngster who had caught Star, grinning cheekily, held out the reins.

Kate smiled weakly back. 'Thanks.'

The man and his wife watched her, interestedly. 'They do say that you should get straight back on, don't they?' suggested the woman helpfully.

Star's back looked a mile high. 'Yes. They do.'

Grimly Kate lifted a foot. Her bones were like jelly – it was all she could do simply to reach the stirrup. Star danced awkwardly sideways. Kate hopped, swearing.

'Want a bunk up?'

'Yes, please.'

The heave the man gave her very nearly shot her off the other side. She could feel the dangerous, nervy movements of the mare. Exerting the last of her strength and will she controlled the upset animal. 'Thank you,' she said again to her rescuers.

'I'd get yourself off home if I were you, dear,' said the woman, kindly. 'You're very pale.'

'Yes, I will.' Still shaking, Kate turned the mare towards the stables and to Miss Jenkins' undoubted – and perfectly justifiable – wrath.

An uncomfortable quarter of an hour later she met, of all people, Jaimie on the stairs.

He stared at her. 'Kate? Are you all right? You're as white as a sheet.'

She leaned on the bannisters, praying that her shaking legs would hold her up just a little longer. 'Yes, I'm okay. I just got myself thrown off a horse, that's all. Stupid.' She suddenly knew that the only alternative to falling was to sit down. She did so, very abruptly, on the stairs.

'Kate . . . !'

'I'm all right. Honest. It's just reaction . . .' She held out her hand to demonstrate its trembling, laughed shakily.

He squatted down beside her, watching her.

'Don't look so worried,' she said, as lightly as she could manage. The trembling was subsiding.

'I thought you didn't ride any more?'

'I don't. Didn't. But I thought I'd have a go . . .'

Almost he smiled. 'And you fell off?'

'Not exactly.' She did not elaborate on that. She was not herself sure of exactly what had happened out there in the park; certainly did not feel like talking about it. She struggled to her feet again.

'Can you manage?'

'Yes. I'm sure I can.'

'Here. Let me give you a hand.' He supported her up the stairs to her door. The shock of their touching affected them both in the same instant. They had not been this close since that last summer night at Screeside. Jaimie drew back from her, his face sombre. 'Kate . . .' he said, simply in the single word a plea, and an acceptance of the impossibility of that plea.

She said nothing. As she opened the door he leaned against the doorjamb, watching her. She did not invite him inside. She turned, waited.

'You know I'm going away again?'

She nodded. 'Jen told me. When are you going?'

'In a month or so. Saudi Arabia.'

She did not move.

'Kate . . . Jen mentioned . . . she said you were thinking of leaving too?'

'Yes.'

'She's terribly upset about it.'

Kate moved her head, avoiding his eyes. 'I'm sorry.'

'Kate . . . it isn't because of us, is it? Because of you and me and . . . and Emily? You don't have to go you know. Especially now. Kate, I couldn't bear to think I'd driven you away . . . with me gone there's no earthly reason why you should leave. Emily understands. I promise you she does. She's told you so herself, hasn't she?'

'Yes.'

'Well, then . . .'

'It isn't that.' Kate left the door and limped painfully into the room. Jaimie followed. 'I'm not going for anyone but me. I feel I have to get away. Not just from you, but from everything here. Everything.' She was staring out of the window to where the long drive, in the darkening evening, made a straight, shadowed line between high, clipped hedges. 'Until now I haven't really been able to make up my mind . . .'

'But now you have?'

She turned, nodded. 'Yes, Jaimie. Now I have. I'm putting the flat on the market tomorrow. I have to go.'

'There's no way to persuade you to stay?'

She shook her head. 'I don't think so.'

'Not even for Jenny?'

Her hesitation was momentary, hardly noticeable. 'Not even for Jenny,' she said, gently regretful.

Over Jaimie's shoulder Stephen watched her, smiling, from his silver frame.

CHAPTER ELEVEN

'It's quite a nice view,' said the woman, whose name Kate could not remember. 'Must be very pretty in the summer?' She leaned to the window, screwing her eyes up in a way that Kate found unreasonably irritating, peering across the mist-shrouded parkland.

'There's a lake across the field there. Behind the trees. I'm afraid you can't actually see it at the moment.'

'A lake? Oh, dear. Is it very deep?'

'I don't know.' Kate's answer was short. The depth of the lake had never been a matter that had much occupied her.

'We've two grandchildren, you see. My daughter's two. They can be . . . a little hard to handle. A lake . . .' the woman's voice trailed off, worriedly.

Best thing for the little blighters,' said her husband, almost the first time he had spoken during the tour of inspection. 'Six foot of water.'

'George!'

George subsided, grinning half-heartedly at Kate. Kate smiled, non-committally. Would they never go?

The woman turned from the window. 'It's all very nice, I must say, and I've always fancied living at the

Hall. But . . . the rooms are a little large, aren't they? Don't you think, George?'

'Yes, dear.'

'And the open fires . . . I'm not sure about them . . . the mess . . .'

It was on the tip of Kate's tongue to ask, in that case, why she had bothered to come to see the flat in the first place, since the open fires were featured prominently in the brochure. With an effort she contained her impatience. How she detested having total strangers looking at her home with eyes that saw nothing but bricks and mortar – 'Perhaps you'd like to think about it?' she asked, helpfully.

The woman gathered up her gloves with evident relief. 'Yes. Of course. That's what we'll do. Go home and think about it. Come along, George.'

George came along. 'Thanks for showing us round, Mrs Richards.'

Kate smiled, and in relief watched their retreating backs down the stairs.

'Kate! What are you doing home at this time of day?' Jenny, in riding clothes, was running lightly down the flight of stairs that led from her front door.

Kate gestured wryly at the departing George and his wife. 'I took the afternoon off. Brought some work home with me. Prospective buyers.'

'Oh.' Jen leaned over the bannisters, pulled a face. 'Are they going to take it?'

'They're going off to think about it.'

Jen followed her into the sitting room. 'Well, really, you know, you ought to let *me* vet everyone who comes. I'm the one who's going to have to live with them, after all.' Her voice was suddenly gloomy. She stretched her hands towards the fire. 'Oh, Kate, are you still absolutely sure about leaving? I do wish you'd stay . . .' she made a swift, half-laughing grimace. 'Sorry. There I go again. I swore I wasn't going to mention it again. But . . . with Jaimie going off too . . .'

'When does he leave?'

'Next week, Thursday.' Jenny wandered to the window. 'Damned fog's closing in. Looks a bit chilly out there, doesn't it?'

'You're going riding?'

'Yes . . . well, I was. Not so sure now. Your fire looks very tempting!'

Kate laughed. 'Why not give it a miss? Stay for a cuppa? You could go out afterwards, if you really wanted to.'

Obviously tempted, Jenny hesitated, then shook her head firmly. 'No. If I get settled in here then I'll certainly never get out, and I've booked Socks from Miss Jenkins. I don't like to let her down. Tell you what . . . I'll brave the elements for half an hour or so, and then come back for a cuppa and a chat. How's that?'

'Done. See you later.'

Jen turned to leave, stopped, surprised. 'Kate?'

'Mm?'

'Stephen's picture . . . the one you always keep on the mantlepiece? It is isn't here?'

'Oh . . . yes. I've been sorting out some bits and pieces, ready to start packing. I thought I might as well pack it away.'

'Oh dear.' Jenny's smile was sad. 'Now I really know you're serious about leaving.'

Kate stood staring into the flames for a long time after she had gone, pondering those words. Despite her resolution, the battle within her still raged. And it was, she knew beyond doubt, with Stephen she battled. His will for her to stay pervaded her life, and stubbornly now she resisted it. She could not in fact tell any longer if her own determination to leave was truly an expression of her own need or simple obstinacy. Stephen had always laughed at that streak of unreasonable mulishness in her nature. 'I do believe you're the only person I know who truly would cut off her nose to spite her face . . .' Was that what she was doing now? She remembered the look on Jen's face a moment ago. Remembered too her resentment of the strangers who had come to see the apartment. The new job was going well. And the journey wasn't too difficult . . .

She pulled herself up short. There she went again.

She walked to the sideboard, opened a drawer. The photograph lay there, waiting for her. She had put it away two days ago, tired of talking to it. Arguing with it. Tired of never getting an answer.

With sudden impatience she banged the drawer shut. From the front of the house came the clatter of hooves as Jenny cantered Socks across the gravel drive. Kate glanced at the clock. Half an hour, Jen had said. Time enough to finish off the work she'd brought home with her, then she'd take the rest of the afternoon off.

She settled herself in front of the fire, with lists of figures and calculator to hand. Absorbed in the task, it was to her surprise a full three-quarters of an hour later that she clicked off the calculator and glanced at her watch. She stood, and stretched, went to the window and peered into the shifting fog. Jenny would be back soon. She went into the kitchen and put the kettle on, stirred the embers of the fire and put another log onto the grate. Jen was bound to be cold when she came in.

She wandered back to the window.

The mist had lifted a little. It wreathed the trees in elfin ribbons of insubstantial grey, drifted across the open land from the lake in deceptive patches, changing perspective and colour like a distorting, misted mirror. Around the lake itself it still hung in a thick, impenetrable curtain. Beyond that curtain Kate saw movement, and for a moment, clearly, she saw Jen, walking her horse at a steady pace out of the trees and into the parkland. Then the fog rolled again, but not before Kate had caught a fleeting glimpse of another rider behind her, shadowy amongst the trees. She screwed up her eyes, trying to focus through the drifting fog. Jen reappeared, unmistakable in her black jacket and light, buff-coloured jodhpurs. As Kate watched she reined in for a moment and half-turned, looking back into the woodland as if waiting, or perhaps listening for someone.

And then he came, through the swirling, thinning mist; a man on a big horse, the converse colours of the riding clothes that he wore complementing Jen's exactly. Foreboding flooded Kate. Her hand crashed against the glass of the window. 'No!'

Jen had turned her mount as the other rider had joined her and was urging the little horse she rode to a canter to keep up with the larger beast.

'Stephen . . . no!'

The two horses were picking up speed now, galloping through the wreathing fog directly towards the house. The will to move, to speak, almost the will to breathe seemed to have deserted Kate entirely. She found herself watching the scene as if it had been a stilled frame from a film, frozen upon a screen of shifting fog. She saw the two horses, tails flying, running flat out towards the hedge-bordered drive, saw that already Jen, an inexperienced horsewoman, had lost control of her mount and was clinging to the animal's mane, completely helpless as it flew across the fog-drenched grass. Beside her, the man rode, his face turned to her, urging her on. And from where Kate stood she saw something else, too. She saw the big van that was coming, too fast, along the sunken drive towards the house. Rooted to the spot she watched Jen's small mount come at the hedge from an impossible angle, slew sideways, crash through, rather than over, the obstacle and tumble, head down and hooves flailing, into the drive, flinging Jen directly into the path of the oncoming van. The bigger horse took the hedge in one graceful, flying leap, gathered itself, jumped clear of the gate on the opposite side and disappeared into the mist.

'My God!' Galvanised at last from her paralysis, Kate found herself running down the stairs two at a time, stumbling, righting herself, dashing on. 'Jen! Oh, please God, No! Not Jen!'

She flew down the drive towards the scene of the accident. There was a bedlam of shouts. A horse was screaming. A small group had already gathered about the still form that sprawled on the wet gravel, one leg at an impossible angle and blood pumping through torn jodhpurs.

'For Christ's sake,' said someone, 'can't someone do something about that horse?'

'She came from nowhere . . . bloody nowhere . . . landed almost on top of me . . .' the van driver was paper white and almost in tears.

Kate pushed her way through the small knot of people, dropped to one knee beside the still figure that lay like a broken doll almost beneath the wheels of the van. 'Jen! Jenny!' Her voice was distraught. Jenny lay as if lifeless, her face drained of colour, her eyes closed.

'Shouldn't touch her, love, if I were you,' said a woman, one hand sympathetically on Kate's shoulder. 'Do more harm than good if you do.'

'But . . .'

'I've sent for the ambulance.' Another woman had joined the group, breathing heavily from her run from the house. 'I saw it happen, and telephoned at once. They're on their way.'

Kate, glancing up, recognised the young woman from the downstairs flat. 'Thank you.' She took

Jenny's limp hand. It was stone cold. 'Shouldn't we at least cover her up?'

'Good idea. Here.' Someone handed her an overcoat. Tenderly she covered Jen's motionless form.

'It wasn't my fault. God knows it wasn't. Came from nowhere, she did. Straight through that hedge like a maniac. I didn't stand a chance . . .' the van driver was shaking with shock.

'I think the horse bolted.' It was the young woman again. 'I was watching from my kitchen window. Something must have scared it. It just took off, like a rocket, from over there . . . near the trees. Poor Mrs Lester just couldn't control it. The damned thing just went at that hedge as if it thought it could fly . . .'

Very slowly Kate lifted her head. 'Did you . . . did you see what happened to the other rider?'

Both the van driver and the woman looked at her blankly.

'There wasn't no other rider,' the man said, flatly.

'But, I thought I saw . . .'

'He's right, Mrs Richards. I saw the whole thing. There was no other rider. Just Mrs Lester. She came from the trees over there, stopped for a moment, and then . . . I don't know . . . perhaps it was the fog . . . the horse just seemed to take fright and bolted . . .'

The dying horse bleated in pain. The van driver turned away from it. 'For God's sake . . . can't we do something for that poor beast?'

'Miss Jenkins has sent for the vet. Now . . . you'd better come inside and have a cup of tea or something. When the ambulance comes, I suppose you'd better go with it, for a check up.' The efficient young woman ushered him away, pausing by Kate's side. 'How is she?'

Kate, still clinging like death to Jen's cold hand, shook her head. 'I don't know.'

From the distance, muffled by the fog, came the sound of sirens. 'That sounds like the ambulance. Will you stay with her?'

'Yes,' Kate said. 'I'll stay.'

Two hours later Jaimie joined Kate at the hospital. His face when he walked into the room where she sat looked haggard with worry and with fear. Kate leapt to her feet. 'How is she? Have you seen her?'

He shook his head, tiredly. 'They're operating. They don't know . . . won't know until later, they said . . .'

They sat in silence in the little, sterile waiting room, unable to exchange even the simplest words of comfort. After a moment Kate asked, 'Are Ben and Emily all right?'

'Yes. The young woman downstairs . . . what's her name? Mrs Stanton, has taken them in for the night. Did you know that poor little Emily was locked into the flat till I came home? Jen had deadlocked the door and accidentally taken the keys out with her . . . Anyway, she's taken it very well. I promised I'd ring as soon as there was any news.' He buried his face in his hands suddenly, 'Oh, God!'

Kate put out a hand to touch him, withdrew it. The miserable silence lengthened. Jaimie stood up and strode restlessly back and forth, filling the small room with his distressed energy. The evening dragged on into night. They drank tea that nearly choked them, attempted to eat sandwiches that might as well have been filled with sawdust. The fog thickened with the night and hung in a dismal curtain at the bare window. When at last a young nurse came in, their two heads jerked as if pulled by the same string.

'Mr Lester.'

'Yes.'

'Would you come this way please? Doctor would like to speak to you.'

The minutes which followed were certainly the longest of Kate's life. She filled them with the odd litany of half-bargaining promises that are so often resorted to in times of stress. Dear God, I'll do anything. Just let Jen be all right. Please . . . let her be all right . . . and all the time, in her head, she saw like a film rerun, over and over, the sight of Stephen galloping beside Jen, urging her on to the Devil's Leap. Stephen, oh Stephen, what have you done?

She started to her feet as the door opened. At first, at the sight of Jaimie's tired, unsmiling face, her heart lurched with fear. 'Jaimie! She isn't . . . ?'

'No! No, it's all right. She badly hurt, but they say she'll be all right. It'll just take time, that's all. She still isn't conscious yet . . . but the doctor said . . . perhaps later . . . if we wanted to wait . . . ?'

'Of course we'll wait.'

He smiled weary thanks at that. Wordlessly Kate went to him, put a supportive arm about him, instilling what comfort she could, loving him more than she ever had, knowing that love transmuted in that moment to the warmth of enduring friendship. They stood so for a long, quiet time. Then Jaimie gently stepped away from her. 'I'll go and phone the children. I promised them I'd let them have any news.'

Much later, they were allowed to see Jen. She lay in a narrow bed whose linen was no whiter than her face, a cage beneath the bedclothes protecting her damaged leg. As they quietly entered the room her eyes flickered open, and she smiled, wanly. 'Hello, you two.'

They stayed for the few minutes they were allowed, and then left. During the drive back to Sheldon Hall neither of them spoke one word.

It was an anxious week before they knew for certain that Jen's damaged leg was mending and the doctor was able to reassure her that, in time, she would walk perfectly normally again. With that promise both her health and her spirits improved rapidly and in a matter of days, bored with being bed-ridden, she had begged a pair of crutches from an understanding doctor and Kate, calling in each evening on her way home from work, grew used to having to hunt for the object of her visit – though after the first few times there was never any doubt about where Jenny would be found; the busy nurses in the children's ward were only too pleased to have an aunty who delighted in reading to their small charges. In no time at all, Jenny had taken the entire ward to her heart.

'Poor little things . . . they're so sweet.' Jenny, her dark eyes soft, looked half her age in her frilled Victorian nightgown, her hair loose and shining about her face. 'The problem is . . . we're running out of books . . .' She glanced, half-laughing, at Kate and put her head on one side, like a child asking a favour of an adult.

Kate held up defensive hands. 'Oh, come on, Jen . . . what do I know about children's books?'

'Well . . . it does seem a shame. I'm sure people must have some that they've just tucked away and forgotten. We really need them . . .'

Kate was well aware of the therapeutic value of this new interest of Jenny's. 'I'll see what I can do,' she said.

Two visits later, Jen's delight at her haul made the effort worthwhile. '*Kate*! How on earth did you do it . . . ?'

'Just asked around here and there. Got a few people organised . . .'

Jen giggled. 'I can imagine.'

'There are more to come. Oh . . . and I approached the local library. They've offered to let the hospital have the pick of their obsolete stock.'

'Kate, you're a genius!' Jenny glanced up to see a white coated figure approaching. 'Doctor Clayton? Doctor Clayton . . .'

Smiling, the doctor joined them. He had, Kate found herself noticing, rather nice eyes in a face that showed distinct signs of needing a couple of days' solid sleep.

'Doctor Clayton . . . this is my friend, Kate . . . she's got these for the children's ward. And we've more coming . . . isn't she clever?'

The doctor smiled tiredly and with interest at Kate and nodded.

'There,' Jenny said with satisfaction when, after the exchange of a few banal pleasantries, the doctor left them, 'that's at least got the two of you introduced.'

Kate stared. 'Jenny Lester . . . what are you talking about?'

Jenny's eyes twinkled. 'He's the nicest man. And he isn't married. I've had my eye on him for you for ages.'

'Jen!'

Jen emptied her hands into the air. 'Don't spoil my fun, Kate, darling . . . what else do I have to think about?'

Christmas came and went, with Jenny improving with every week. As the time came closer when she knew she would be allowed home, her spirits rose. In the weeks since she had introduced them she watched the careful friendship which blossomed between Kate and Geoff Clayton with a proprietorial satisfaction.

'Now, come on, Kate . . . when are you going out with him?'

Kate smiled a small, exasperated smile. 'He hasn't asked me.'

'That's only because he knows you'll say no.'

Kate did not reply. The pale January sunshine fell

in bright shafts across Jenny's bed.

'Jen?'

Jenny was still smiling. 'Yes?'

Kate sought the words to broach a subject that she dreaded to discuss, but which had haunted her through these past weeks. 'The . . . the accident,' she said hesitantly. 'You've never spoken about it. Never told me exactly what happened?'

Jen hesitated. A faint furrow had appeared between her dark brows.

'I'm sorry,' Kate said hastily, '. . . if you don't want to talk about it?'

'No. It isn't that. It's just . . . truth to tell . . . I find it hard to remember myself exactly what did happen.' She folded her hands on the spotless cover. 'I was riding through the woods by the lake. You remember how foggy it was?'

Kate nodded.

'I thought . . . I thought I heard something. Someone . . .'

'Someone?'

'Yes. A voice. A man's voice, calling. I stopped, but there wasn't anyone there. Then . . . I came out of the woods and into the field. I remember that the mist lifted a little and I saw you, waiting at your lighted window. Then I heard it again. The voice, calling. You know how fog can distort sound . . . it must have been someone over by the lake . . . though it actually sounded much closer.'

'Was it . . . calling you?' Kate asked, carefully.

'No. In fact, I couldn't really hear it properly at all.

Oddly enough, if I had to guess, I think I'd say it was someone calling your name. Kate. Or . . . perhaps it was "Hey . . ." I don't know. All I know is that when I stopped to look back something spooked that damned horse, and I just couldn't hold him.'

'You didn't see what it was?'

Jen shook her head. On her face was a faintly puzzled expression. Her fingers fidgeted a little with the bedcover. 'I do remember one thing that seems very strange.'

'What's that?'

'When I think about it . . . I must be wrong . . . but I seem to remember the oddest feeling of . . . of excitement. Of exhilaration, almost. Happiness isn't too strong a word. It's ridiculous of course when you think of what happened. I should have been terrified. I suppose a part of me was terrified . . . but . . .' She shook her head, perplexed. 'I'm sorry. It must sound very stupid.'

Kate shook her head, unspeaking.

Jenny let out a long slow breath. Dust motes danced in the sunshine. Jen lifted her head, smiling. 'Did Jaimie tell you that they may let me home in a week or so?'

'Yes, he did.'

'I can't wait to get out of here. Although . . . it's going to be a bit difficult I suppose. With Jaimie gone again, I mean.' She traced the pattern on the counterpane with a small white finger. 'You know he has to go away again? He's very upset about it . . . having to leave me . . .' Her voice was a little uncertain. 'But they won't hold the job for him for ever . . . they've been very good so far . . . so now he has to go. We'll need the money more than ever now, with home helps and things for a little while . . .' She nibbled her lip, smiled over-brightly. 'I'm sure we'll be able to manage, though.'

Kate had been waiting to break her own news. Now seemed a better time than most. She took Jen's fidgeting hand in her own. 'We'll manage together, if you like.' She shrugged a little, smiling. 'If it won't disappoint you not to have new neighbours after all, that is?'

As the meaning of the words came to Jenny she smiled brilliantly, her eyes shining. 'Oh . . . darling Kate! . . . how marvellous!' The smile broadened to a grin as a tall shadow fell across the bed.

'Good news?' asked Geoff Clayton.

'Very.' All innocence, Jenny smiled up at him. 'For all of us I'd say.'

After he had gone, Jenny giggled happily. Kate cocked a suspicious eyebrow.

'What's so funny?'

'Nothing. Nothing at all.' Jenny grinned from the white-coated departing back to Kate's face. 'I was just planning my first dinner party, that's all.'

When Kate let herself in to the flat at Sheldon House, the first thing that she noticed was that Stephen's photograph, in its silver frame, was back in pride of place on the mantlepiece. She stood stock still, staring at it.

'I put it back,' Emily said, from the doorway. 'You don't mind do you? I thought he'd been in disgrace for long enough.'

Kate walked across the room, her eyes fixed on the photograph, a frown on her face, 'I . . .'

'Oh, please, Kate, we mustn't be too angry with him.' Emily had come to stand beside her. Her voice was soft and urgent.

'Angry with him?' asked Kate, carefully.

'For what he did.'

Kate turned to look at her.

'I saw him too,' the girl said, simply.

Kate could think of absolutely nothing to say.

'But Kate . . . dear Kate . . . can't you see? He's so sorry now. He is. I know it. He only did it because he had to find a way to make you stay. You were going away, and he couldn't stand that . . .'

Kate shook her head, nonplussed. There was a long moment's silence.

'And you aren't going away now, are you?' The quiet words were barely a question. 'Not with Mum needing you so?'

'No,' Kate said, 'I'm not.'

Emily's eyes flicked to the picture. 'There,' she said, 'I told you so, didn't I?' Then, more brightly, to Kate, 'There's some tea made in the kitchen. Would you like some?'

'Yes. Please.' Still more than a little bemused Kate watched the girl from the room before, very slowly, she took the picture from the mantlepiece, very gently touched a finger to the eternally smiling mouth. In the kitchen, Emily was singing softly. *'In Scarlet Town, where I was born . . . There was a fair maid dwelling . . .'*

If Emily can forgive you, then I guess I can. Perhaps, after all, the child knows more about love than we ever did?

'Kate? Tea up . . .'

'Coming,' she said.